THE HOUNDS OF HADES

Three of the squad were still standing. A man with a scar on his chin raised his M-16 to shoot, but took a slug in his right eye that spun him completely around and stopped him in his tracks.

Only two left. Both were within six feet of Blade, one to his left, the other his right. With consummate skill, Blade raised the knives overhead and threw. The blades glistened in the sunlight as they flew into the chests of their respective targets. Twelve inches of cold steel were imbedded to the hilt in each Hound. Both men looked astonished; both dropped their machine guns and clutched at the Bowies; both gawked at Blade in amazement for a moment; and both sank into eternity without uttering a sound.

Also in the *Endworld* series:

ENDWORLD

#18:
MEMPHIS RUN
DAVID ROBBINS

LEISURE BOOKS   **L**   NEW YORK CITY

Dedicated to—
Judy, Joshua, and Shane
in eternal affection.
To Herman Brix, who did it best.
And to the memory of Elvis.

A LEISURE BOOK®

November 1989

Published by

Dorchester Publishing Co., Inc.
276 Fifth Avenue
New York, NY 10001

Copyright © 1989 by David Robbins

Printed in the United States of America.

CHAPTER ONE

"Did you see that?" the girl asked.

"See what?" responded the lean man in buckskins. His keen blue eyes scanned the lush foliage ahead as his hands dropped to the pearl-handled Colt Python revolvers strapped around his narrow waist. The westerly breeze stirred his blond hair.

"I saw something," the girl insisted.

Frowning, his sweeping blond mustache curling downward, the gunman took several strides in front of the child. "What was it? Another blasted mutant?"

"I don't know."

"I'm gettin' fed up with havin' to blow a mutant away every fifty miles or so," the gunman commented.

"I don't think it was a mutant," the girl said. "It looked like a man."

"Are you sure, Chastity?"

The girl walked up to the gunman and tugged on his right pants leg. "Would I lie to you, Daddy?" She wore a blue jump suit in need of a thorough washing. Her shoulder-length blonde hair framed a face of angelic innocence, and her blue eyes looked at the man accusingly.

"No, princess. I reckon you wouldn't," the gunman admitted. "How far away was this varmint?"

"There," Chastity said, pointing at a cluster of trees a

hundred yards distant.

"Something wrong, Hickok?" inquired a newcomer behind them in a deep, resonant voice.

"Or is it time for another potty break, Daddy?" added another man with a hint of humor in his tone.

Hickok turned and stared critically at the second speaker, a small, wiry man dressed all in black with a katana scabbard aligned under his belt on his left hip and the corner of a brown pouch visible behind his right hip. His black attire complemented his dark hair and eyes. "Are you makin' fun of me, Rikki?" Hickok demanded.

The Family's supreme martial artist kept a straight face. "Would I stoop to teasing you? The code of Bushido does not permit a perfected swordmaster to indulge in sarcasm."

Hickok made a snorting noise. "If words were bull manure, I'd be in it up to my waist! You're worse than that mangy Injun."

"What mangy Injun?" Chastity interjected.

The gunman gazed down at her. "One of my best buddies is an Indian named Geronimo. He's a Warrior, just like me."

Chastity nodded. "Oh. That's right. You've talked about him before. You must like him a lot."

"For a six-year-old, you're pretty sharp," Hickok remarked. Then he sighed. "Yeah. I miss Geronimo heaps. But don't ever tell him that."

"Why not?" Chastity questioned.

"I don't want him to think I'm gettin' mushy in my old age," Hickok said.

"You're not old," Chastity insisted.

The fourth member of their quartet cleared his throat. "If you don't mind, I'd like to keep moving unless there was a reason for stopping."

Hickok faced the man with the deep voice, a towering giant whose bulging muscles served as a visible testimony to his prodigious strength. "Chastity saw something or someone up yonder," he reported.

"Why didn't you say so?" asked the titan, a seven-foot

colossus attired in a black leather vest, green fatigue pants, and black combat boots. Suspended from his belt on each hip was a Bowie knife in a brown sheath. His gray eyes narrowed and he ran his right hand through his dark, wind-blown hair. He scrutinized the terrain in their path, then looked at the girl. "What did you see?"

"A man, I think. He went from tree to tree," she answered, and gestured at the stand of trees.

"Did he see us?" the giant probed.

"He was looking at us, Blade," Chastity replied.

Blade rested his hands on his Bowies. "*Now* what?"

"I'll check it out," Hickok offered.

"Allow me," Rikki interjected, and grinned at the gunman. "Daddy should stay here with Chastity."

"Go," Blade said to the martial artist. Then he added an afterthought: "Be careful."

"Will do," Rikki promised, jogging off.

"I like Ricky-Picky-Daffy," Chastity declared. "He's nice."

"How many times do I have to tell you?" Hickok responded. "His name is Rikki-Tikki-Tavi, and he took his name from a mongoose."

"I still don't get it," Chastity admitted. "How come you don't keep the names your mommies and daddies give you?"

"I've explained it before," Hickok noted. "At the place we come from, a compound called the Home, everyone goes through a Naming ceremony when they turn sixteen. The man who built our Home, the man we call the Founder of our Family, started the Naming ceremony. He wanted us to go through the history books in our big library and find any name we liked as our own. It was his way of trying to make sure we stayed in touch with our roots, so to speak."

"I don't understand," Chastity said.

"Don't fret your noggin' over it," Hickok stated. "I'll explain the whole deal again when you're seven."

Chastity pursed her thin lips for a moment. "Where did your name come from?"

"Mine? Hickok was the name of a great gunfighter," Hickok detailed. "He lived centuries ago. His full name was James Butler Hickok, and he was one of the deadliest gunfighters who ever lived."

"Is that why you picked his name?" Chastity inquired.

"Not because he was deadly," Hickok said. "But because he was the best at what he did, yet he never used his skill to deliberately hurt folks unless they had it comin'. He was a lawman in the Old West."

"What happened to him?"

"He was shot in the back of the head by a mangy, yellow coyote by the name of McCall," Hickok disclosed. "McCall was too yellow to take Hickok on man to man in an honest shoot-out." He paused. "Everyone knew Hickok was unbeatable. The only way to get him was in the back."

Chastity's expression became a mirror of concern. "You won't let that happen to you!"

"Jack McCall bit the dust ages ago."

"Not him. But another bad man might try to shoot you in the back," Chastity said in alarm. She impulsively reached out and hugged him around the knees. "Don't let anyone kill you. I don't want to lose another daddy."

Hickok gently placed his left hand on the top of her head. "Don't worry, princess. No one will ever plug me in the back."

Chastity squeezed tightly. "I hope not. I love you."

The gunman swallowed hard. "I'm fond of you too, little one." Eager to change the subject, he glanced up. "Rikki is gettin' close to those trees."

Chastity released his knees and turned. "He'd better watch out."

"Was the man you saw armed?" Blade asked.

"I don't know," she replied.

Blade gazed at the gunman. "I'm beginning to believe you're right."

"About what?" Hickok responded.

"About returning to the Home," Blade said. "If our map

is accurate, we should be within forty miles or less of Memphis.''

"If Memphis is still there,'' Hickok observed. "Maybe it was hit during the war.''

"We'll find out,'' Blade declared. "In any event, we need transportation capable of reaching Minnesota. We've been walking for weeks, and we have over twelve hundred miles to go. Here it is, August already, and at the rate we're traveling we won't reach the Home until next August.''

"So what was I right about?'' Hickok asked.

"About acquiring transportation,'' Blade mentioned.

"You mean when I said we should steal it?'' Hickok inquired.

The giant nodded. "We may have no choice.'' He sighed sadly. "I miss Jenny and Gabe.''

"You miss your missus and young'un, and I miss mine,'' Hickok concurred. "All I think about is Sherry and Ringo.''

"And me?'' Chastity interjected hopefully.

"And you,'' Hickok said with a smile.

"I hope Mrs. Hickok and Ringo like me,'' Chastity stated.

"They will,'' Hickok assured her. "And call my missus Sherry. Mrs. Hickok sounds sort of stuffy.''

Chastity's features abruptly conveyed an inner melancholy. "I wish my mommy and daddy were alive.''

Hickok and Blade exchanged glances.

"I'm happy that you're my new daddy,'' Chastity said to the gunman, "but I want my mommy and daddy back.''

"They've gone to a better world,'' Blade said.

"Where?''

Blade pursed his lips and watched Rikki enter the forest ahead. What could he say to alleviate her remorse? He tried to recall conversations he'd had with his son along similar lines. "Our Elders teach us that death is just the way we get from this world to a higher spiritual level. Your mommy and daddy have gone on ahead of you and will be waiting for you when you arrive.''

"Mommy told me we go to heaven when we die,'' Chastity

said. "Will mommy and daddy know me in heaven?"

"I believe so, yes," Blade affirmed.

"I can't wait to get there," Chastity asserted.

"Whoa, princess. There's no rush," Hickok remarked. "We all pass on when the time comes."

"When will my time come?"

"We have no way of knowin'," Hickok said. "So we should live our lives to the fullest until we do kick the bucket. There's no sense in worryin' over when our number will be called. And there's no sense in hurryin' it along, either. What will be, will be."

Blade chuckled. "I had no idea you're such a philosopher. You should teach a class at the Home on the meaning of life. I'll write your petition to the Elders."

"I'm not qualified to teach a schooling class, and you know it," Hickok declared.

"Do you have a school at your Home?" Chastity queried.

"Yep," Hickok answered. "The young'uns are taught by our Elders in one of our concrete bunkers. There are all kinds of classes."

"Like what?"

"Horticulture, agriculture, weaving, history, math, geography," Hickok said. "You name it, the Elders will teach it."

"Did they teach you to be a Warrior?"

"One of them was my instructor," Hickok responded. "The Warriors are given extra instruction to prepare them for the job."

"Like what?"

Hickok looked at Blade. "Why is it kids ask so many questions?" Then he turned back to Chastity. "Warriors must constantly train to stay sharp. I practice with my Colts every chance I get. Blade does the same with his pigstickers."

"What's a pigsticker?"

"He means my Bowie knives," Blade explained.

"Why does he call them pigstickers?" Chastity wanted to know.

"Haven't you noticed how Hickok uses funny words?" Blade asked.

Chastity nodded. "He uses them all the time."

"And do you know why?" Blade queried.

"Yeah. Rikki told me it's because my new daddy has a warped brain."

"What?" Hickok snapped, staring at the tree line. "When did he say that?"

"A couple of days ago. Why? Isn't it true?" Chastity queried.

"If anything is warped around here, it's Rikki's sense of humor," Hickok stated. "My brain is as normal as anyone else's."

"Then why do you use so many funny words?"

The gunman crouched and tenderly touched his right forefinger to her chin. "Out of habit, I reckon. I started using words from the Old West when I was a whippersnapper, and the habit stuck. I'm partial to the way of life they lived way back then. When I was little, I wished I'd been born a cowboy or a marshal in a frontier town. All my childhood heroes came from Western books. Now Blade was different. He liked these books about a man who went around swingin' in trees with nothin' on but his underwear. This guy could talk to monkeys and elephants and he liked livin' in the jungle. So who's more warped? Blade or me?"

"You."

"Me? Why?"

"Blade doesn't talk like a monkey," Chastity said, and hugged him again, this time about the neck. "I don't care how you talk. I love you anyway."

Blade saw the gunman's face redden and he smiled. "Hickok, I've got to hand it to you. If you hadn't adopted her, I would've done so myself. She's a peach."

Chastity let go and glanced up at the giant. "Really?"

"Really and truly," Blade assured her.

Hickok stood. "You'll like our Home, princess. A twenty-foot-high brick wall keeps out all the mutants and other riffraff. You won't need to worry about something tryin' to kill you every two minutes. And the folks are as nice as could be. There are lots of young'uns your age to play with.''

"When will we get to the Home?"

"Soon, I hope," Hickok said. "My feet are—"

Blade held aloft his right hand, interrupting the gunfighter. "Quiet!"

"What is it?" Chastity asked.

"Hush, little one," Hickok whispered. He cocked his head, listening, and a second later heard an unusual, metallic coughing noise coming from the trees.

Blade took three strides forward. "It sounds like a motor trying to turn over."

"I've got a bad feeling about this," Hickok declared.

"Let's hide," Chastity suggested.

The noise was repeated, only louder and lasting twice as long before sputtering into silence.

"Where's Rikki?" Blade inquired of no one in particular.

"Shouldn't we hide?" Chastity prompted.

"You take care of the princess," Hickok proposed. "I'll go find Daffy."

Before Blade could respond, there was a thunderous roar accompanied by the crashing of saplings and the crushing of underbrush, and a green behemoth lumbered from cover in the stand of trees and rattled toward them.

"It's a half-track!" Hickok exclaimed.

"Hide!" Blade ordered, turning and starting for the woods 40 yards to their rear.

Just as the half-track opened up with its .50-caliber machine gun.

CHAPTER TWO

Rikki-Tikki-Tavi approached the trees cautiously. He suppressed an impulse to yawn and gripped the hilt of his katana with his right hand. The days and weeks of sustained tension, he realized, were beginning to take their toll. No matter how superbly conditioned the Warriors might be, they were not machines; they could not function at their peak level, at full alertness, 24 hours a day, every day, without a letup. And they were being forced to do just that. During the day they had to be constantly on guard for animals, mutants, and human foes. At night their sleep was fitful. Each one was required to take a three-hour shift tending the campfire, and those attempting to catch a few hours of badly needed slumber were continually awakened by snarls and shrieks emanating from the darkness.

He would be glad when they reached the Home.

The forest ahead seemed ominously still.

Rikki slowed, searching for indications of movement. His concentration flagged, and he thought of his friends. Hickok had performed a noble deed in giving a home to Chastity. The poor girl had been devastated after her parents were killed by Terminators from Atlanta. The Family would receive her with open arms.

What was that?

The martial artist paused, his eyes focusing on a dense

thicket to his left. Had something moved? He grasped the katana tighter and advanced to the tree line.

No birds were chirping.

No insects were buzzing.

The woods were like a tomb.

Why?

Rikki mentally debated whether to continue or return to Blade and report. But report what? He chided himself for unnecessary nervousness and walked into the timber. Blade had displayed periodic bouts of uncharacteristic impatience during their trek, and Rikki did not want to contribute to the head Warrior's testiness by failing to discharge his duties. Ever since Miami and their battle with the drug lords, Blade had been on a short fuse. Normally, the giant maintained a cool head even in the direst of situations.

So why the change?

A twig snapped to the right.

Rikki crouched and pivoted. His skin was prickling, as if his sixth sense, an attribute honed after years of combat, was trying to warn him that unseen eyes were watching him. If so, whoever they were, they were good. He couldn't see any sign of enemies lurking in the vegetation.

As it turned out, they weren't lurking in the vegetation— they were lurking *above* it.

Annoyed at his unease, filled with self-reproach over not centering his attention solely on the task at hand, Rikki moved farther from the field where his friends awaited his return. He was beginning to think his imagination was getting the better of him when someone sneezed.

Directly overhead.

Rikki was passing under the spreading branches of a mighty hardwood, and he glanced up in surprise, the katana a gleaming streak as it flashed from its scabbard. But as quick as he was, he was not quick enough.

They dropped on him from their perches of concealment, a half-dozen figures dressed in black: black shirts, black pants, and black boots. They were armed with an assortment of weaponry. Some bore rifles or machine guns over their shoulders, and most had holstered handguns. All were clean-shaven, their hair closely cropped. They did not shout or chatter. Silently, efficiently, they struck.

Rikki arced his katana into the abdomen of the nearest falling form, the ancient blade cutting deep into the man's stomach, slicing fabric and flesh. The man grunted and doubled over as he landed, clutching at the blood and organs spewing forth. Rikki put him out of his misery with a neck slash, crimson spurting everywhere as the man toppled to the grass.

The rest closed on the martial artist.

In the first fleeting seconds of the fight, Rikki realized his antagonists weren't even trying to use their holstered or shouldered firearms.

They wanted him alive!

A man charged from the left, and Rikki whipped his katana across the figure's chest. Strong hands clasped his right arm before he could strike a second time, and he slammed his right elbow into the face of the beefy form restraining him.

Three others piled on the Warrior.

Rikki felt hands on both of his arms, and a sturdy head-lock was being applied from the rear. He drove his head backwards and was rewarded by the crunch of his cranium against nostrils or teeth. The headlock was relinquished, leaving the two on his arms. He suddenly dropped to his right knee and twisted to the left, causing the black-garbed opponent on his right to stumble forward, momentarily off balance. The man's hold on Rikki's forearm slackened, and the martial artist drove his right hand up and in, using a Tegatana blow, a handsword strike, the outer edge of his calloused hand connecting with his adversary's ribs. There was a sharp crack and the man staggered off.

The one on the left was clinging to the Warrior's sword arm for dear life.

His right hand rigid, his thumb tucked tightly against the inner edge, his fingers slightly apart and curving, Rikki twisted, delivering a Tegatana-sakotsu-uchi, a handsword collarbone chop, to the man's right side. Again there was a pronounced snap. The man grimaced and stepped away.

He was free!

Rikki turned, intending to race to the field and warn Blade and Hickok. There might be more of these commandos nearby, and they were obviously disciplined and well-trained. No one had cried out.

"Going somewhere?" demanded a gruff voice behind him. "The fun is just beginning."

Rikki whirled, his sword at the ready.

"I'm impressed, pip-squeak, and it takes a lot to impress me," said the newcomer. He was tall, almost as tall as Blade, but much leaner. On the shoulders of his black shirt was a pair of small gold insignia. His face was pear-shaped, his forehead wide and sloping. A chipped upper tooth was revealed when he smiled. "The King will be pleased with you. Very pleased." He hefted an unusual object in his left hand.

Rikki tensed as more forms materialized from hiding, dropping from nearby trees. He glanced at the object in the tall man's hand, a black, oblong affair with a pair of pointed tips projecting from the front end.

One of the others walked over to the tall man and saluted. "Sir, the girl and the two men haven't moved."

"We'll take them in a minute, Captain."

"Yes, sir, General."

The General grinned at the Warrior. "This will be quite a haul. The girl will be a special treat."

Rikki had heard enough. Warning his companions was imperative. He started to spin, his eyes on the tall man.

There was a distinct click as the General pressed a button on the object in his left hand. One of the small tips, trailing a slim, thread-like wire, shot from the oblong affair.

Reacting instinctively, Rikki attempted to dodge to the right. His lightning reflexes, in this instance, failed him. The tiny dart speared into his left shoulder, causing a fleeting, stinging sensation, and he wondered why the General had employed such a ineffectual weapon.

The answer came with shocking intensity.

Rikki's entire body was racked by an inexplicable jolt of incredible magnitude. He lost all ability to control his muscles and fell to the ground, his arms and legs quivering in torment, his features twitching. The katana slipped from his limp fingers. Vertigo engulfed him.

"Bind him," the General ordered with a snap of his fingers.

A trio of men in black promptly complied, using handcuffs to secure the Warrior's wrists. One of them produced another set, which was applied to Rikki's ankles. He then removed the brown pouch, letting the scabbard drop, and refastened the Warrior's belt.

"Stand aside," the General commanded, moving closer and smirking triumphantly. "How do you feel, pip-squeak?"

Rikki tried to reply, but his mouth refused to cooperate. The trembling in his limbs, though, was slowly subsiding.

"This stun gun does the trick every time," the General remarked as he leaned over and extracted the dart from the Warrior's shoulder. "You'll be as good as new in five minutes." He straightened and pressed a different button. The thin line began to retract into the oblong object. "We ambushed a Technic trade convoy about two years ago between Chicago and St. Louis. There was a crate of these on one of the trucks."

The one who had saluted came nearer. "Your orders for the girl and the two others, General Thayer?"

"Send the half-track and a squad out after them," General Thayer directed. "The half-track should scare them shitless. They'll be easy to take. Lead the squad yourself."

"Yes, sir," the captain said. He saluted and hurried away.

Rikki saw the general insert the tiny dart into a hole in the stun gun as the line fully rewound. The officer slid the weapon into a custom-made holster on his left hip.

"What kind of sword is this?" General Thayer inquired,

retrieving the katana. He studied the blade, admiring the craftsmanship. "It looks old. Real old. I think I'll add this one to my collection." So saying, he leaned down and scooped up the scabbard from the ground. "You won't be needing this anymore either."

Rikki watched helplessly as his cherished possession was confiscated. He endeavored to strain against the handcuffs binding his wrists in front of him, but the effort was wasted. Just then, from somewhere beyond his range of vision, a motor sputtered and died. The noise was repeated, and on the third try there was a great crashing and rumbling.

"Your friends will be my prisoners within minutes," General Thayer gloated. He motioned at one of the men.

"Yes, sir," the man said, coming over, an HK-33 over his left arm.

"Carry this one to my jeep," General Thayer instructed. "Stand guard over him while I tend to his friends."

The man in black saluted. "Yes, sir. Right away."

"Thank you, Sergeant Boynton." With a curt nod, the general walked in the direction of the field.

"You, you, and you," Sergeant Boynton said, pointing at three others. "Carry this scumbag to the general's jeep."

Rikki was lifted and borne to the northwest. He heard a machine gun cut loose, and he closed his eyes and clenched his teeth, furious at himself. Blade, Hickok, and Chastity were endangered because of his blunder. He should have perceived the trap. His lack of rest, his overtaxed vitality, was no excuse.

Sergeant Boynton, gazing at the Warrior's face, laughed. "Don't feel so bad, scumbag. The Hounds of Hades are invincible."

With a supreme effort of sheer willpower, Rikki managed to speak. "The Hounds of Hades?" he croaked.

"Nifty name, isn't it?" Sergeant Boynton said. "The King came up with it. He wanted us to have a name that would strike fear into the hearts of our enemies. Those were his own words." He chuckled. "The Hounds of Hades has a real ring."

Rikki listened to the machine gun chatter, wishing the firing would stop. It did, and a few seconds later resumed.

"Where are you from?" Boynton asked.

The Warrior refused to respond.

"Suit yourself, turkey," Sergeant Boynton stated with a shrug. "The King will get the info out of you. But you must not be from this area, or you'd know all about us. We have a heavy rep. Hell, we've even beaten Technic goons and Leather Knights a few times. We're one hundred and twenty strong and growing."

Rikki, perplexed by the sergeant's comments, heard the machine gun abruptly cease. What had happened? Surely Blade, Hickok, and Chastity were alive? After all, the general had indicated he wanted them as prisoners. "Are you a professional mercenary?" he queried absently.

"No way, man," Sergeant Boynton answered. "I was drifting from town to town, barely staying alive like everybody else, when I waltzed into Memphis and met the King. That was about three years ago. I was there at the beginning. Thayer—sorry—General Thayer trained us. He made us what we are today."

"Kidnappers."

"No, butt-head. An army."

"An army of kidnappers," Rikki said, relieved his vocal chords were functioning normally again.

"Are you pushing for a fat lip?" Sergeant Boynton demanded. "You're the one who violated our territorial boundary. We'll take you to the King and he'll decide what to do with you. Thank your lucky stars you're not a Technic or a Leather Knight. They're usually executed immediately."

Rikki knew about the Technics and the Leather Knights. The former were a society of autocratic technocrats in Chicago. The Leather Knights were a biker gang controlling St. Louis. Both had fought the Warriors. He opened his

mouth to speak, but the booming of revolvers from the
direction of the field arrested his attention. Hickok?

"Here we are," Sergeant Boynton announced as they
arrived at a clearing containing two parked jeeps.

The trio bearing the Warrior moved toward the nearest
vehicle. One Hound held Rikki around the knees, the second
around the waist, and the third supported his shoulders. They
conveyed him to the rear of the topless jeep and uncere-
moniously dumped him in the back.

Rikki thudded against a spare tire and a gas can, landing
on his back.

Sergeant Boynton leaned on the jeep. "It sounds like one
of your pals is putting up a fight. Pretty stupid, if you ask
me. Our half-track will make mincemeat out of him."

"You don't know my friend," Rikki said.

"Get real. A handgun can't stop a half-track," Boynton
declared, and laughed.

As if in confirmation of the noncom's statement, from the
southeast arose a ghastly shriek.

A child in anguish.

CHAPTER THREE

With its .50-caliber machine gun blasting, the green half-track clanked toward the two Warriors and the girl.

Hickok scooped Chastity into his arms and raced on Blade's heels, heading for the cover of the woods at the opposite end of the field. He expected to be outdistanced easily by his friend; Blade's stride was twice the average. Instead, the head Warrior intentionally slowed. "Keep going, pard!" Hickok shouted. "You can make it!"

"I'm not leaving you," Blade said.

The gunman glanced over his right shoulder. For an antiquated armored vehicle with caterpillar treads on its rear wheels, the half-track was barreling toward them at a rapid clip. There was no way they could outrun the contraption. If any of them were to escape, then one had to make a sacrifice, take a risk. "Here!" he yelled, and shoved Chastity into Blade's arms.

Taken unawares, Blade reflexively grabbed the girl. "What—!"

Hickok spun and sprinted at the half-track.

"Daddy!" Chastity wailed.

Blade halted. "Hickok!"

Ignoring them, the gunman was going all out, his arms and legs pumping.

Blade glanced at the half-track and saw the trooper or

soldier in black manning the machine gun swivel the piece
to cover the gunfighter. The initial bursts from the .50 had
fallen short of the Warriors, and the first rounds aimed in
Hickok's direction also fell short by several yards, stitching
the earth and sending clumps of turf flying. Blade recognized
the machine gunner had given Hickok a warning burst. Incredibly, the gunman paid it no heed.

"Daddy! No!" Chastity cried.

What the hell was Hickok doing? Blade dashed for the
trees. Once Chastity was out of harm's way, he could lend
assistance to the gunfighter. He looked over his left shoulder
as he ran and watched the tableau unfold.

The machine gunner, apparently surprised by the
gunman's failure to stop, fired a hasty burst at the Warrior's
feet.

His eyes widening in horror, Blade inadvertently halted
as Hickok went down. The gunman clutched at his chest and
pitched onto his stomach.

"*No!*" Chastity screamed at the top of her lungs, the word
coming out as a strangled screech.

The half-track swerved to bypass the prone Warrior,
revealing eleven men in black following the vehicle with
rifles and machine guns in their hands. Two of the squad
jogged to Hickok and hoisted him by the arms. The gunfighter's head slumped on his chest.

"They killed my new daddy!" Chastity exclaimed.

Blade sped for the woods.

"Halt!" one of the men in black ordered.

Well-aimed rounds from the .50 were sent zinging over
the giant's head as additional incentive.

Blade drew up short.

"Go!" Chastity urged, kicking her legs.

"We can't outrun a bullet," Blade said.

The squad of men in black hastened nearer as the half-
track executed a wide U-turn, the driver positioning the
vehicle between the giant and the woods, cutting off Blade's
retreat.

"My daddy," Chastity stated sadly, sniffling.

"Don't touch those knives," the leader of the squad barked when he was ten feet off.

"Don't harm the girl," Blade said.

"Worry about your own hide, stranger," the leader responded. "I'm Captain Ludvin of the Hounds of Hades. You are under arrest for trespassing in our territory."

"I didn't see any signs telling us to keep out," Blade mentioned.

"Ignorance is no excuse," Captain Ludvin snapped. His men ringed the giant, their rifles and machine guns trained on his chest. "You will come with us."

"I don't have any choice," Blade commented.

"No, you don't," Captain Ludvin confirmed. He motioned with the Valmet M-76 he was holding. "Let's go."

On the far side of the field over a dozen forms in black were waiting, with an exceptionally tall figure standing in the center. Halfway across were the pair with Hickok, at the spot where he fell, likewise awaiting the squad and the half-track.

One of the Hounds took the giant's knives.

"Don't lose them," Blade said. "I may want them back soon."

Captain Ludvin snorted. "Fat chance. Now move your ass."

Blade walked between Ludvin and the man carrying the Bowies. He gazed at Hickok, his mouth turned down.

Chastity weeped softly on his left shoulder.

"The one in the buckskins was a moron," Captain Ludwin remarked. "What was he trying to prove?"

"Don't talk that way about my daddy!" Chastity said.

"Shut your mouth, brat," Captain Ludvin responded.

Tears streaming down her cheeks, Chastity bunched her fists and glared at the officer. "If I was bigger, I'd show you! You're a mean man!"

Ludvin raised his right arm, about to smack the girl, but a glance at the giant's expression deterred him. "You're not worth the bother," he muttered angrily, and lowered his arm.

"You—you—" Chastity said, apparently unable to find the word she wanted. "You cow chip!"

Captain Ludvin laughed.

"Where's my other friend?" Blade inquired, restraining his temper with a monumental effort.

"You mean the one in the fancy pajamas?" Captain Ludvin replied.

"Those clothes were tailor-made by our Weavers," Blade remarked. "The style is patterned after the type of uniform worn by Chinese martial artists before the Big Blast."

"Before World War Three?" Ludvin queried. "How would you know what the clothes back then were like?"

"From photographs in books in our library."

Captain Ludvin paused and his men halted. "Your people have a library?"

Blade nodded.

"The King will be very interested in this," Ludvin said. "He's a real book nut."

"Who is this King?" Blade asked.

"You'll meet him soon enough. Keep moving," Ludvin directed, and walked forward.

"You still haven't told me what happened to my other friend," Blade noted.

"He's in our custody," Captain Ludvin disclosed. "Just like you."

"Do the Hounds of Hades capture everyone who enters their so-called territory?" Blade probed.

"Everyone entering our territory is taken to the King for interrogation," the officer said. "And for your information, anything within fifty miles of Memphis is ours." He grinned. "One day we'll have much more."

"Big plans, huh?" Blade quipped sarcastically.

"If you only knew."

They were within 20 feet of the duo supporting Hickok.

"We'll leave the moron for the vultures and the mutants," Captain Ludvin mentioned. He stared at the revolvers in the gunman's holsters. "And I think I'll ask the general if I can have one of those. Colts, are they?"

"Yes," Blade answered softly.

Chastity was sniffling again.

The squad stopped five feet away. Behind them, the half-track braked. The machine gunner was resting his elbows on the .50-caliber in the open rear bed.

"Is he dead?" Captain Ludvin inquired of the duo.

They looked at one another.

"We didn't check him, sir," replied the Hound on the right.

"Didn't check him?" Ludvin declared. "You didn't even feel his pulse?"

"It didn't seem like he was breathing," the Hound on the left said. "So we didn't bother."

"You incompetent jackasses!" Captain Ludvin stated. "You'll receive thirty lashes for this!"

"How about some lead instead?" interjected the object of their controversy, startling the duo by wrenching his arms from their grasp and taking several strides backwards. "You mangy varmints."

For the span of a second no one moved. The Hounds were caught napping, with most holding their weapons pointed carelessly at the ground. On the half-track the machine gunner gaped at the man he'd "killed."

Chastity precipitated the inevitable blood bath. "Daddy!" she cried happily, and her voice galvanized the men around her to action.

The Hounds endeavored to bring their rifles and machine guns into play as Captain Ludvin bellowed, "Get him!"

Hickok's hands were a blur as the Pythons cleared leather. His first two shots took out the stunned duo, a slug penetrating each Hound's forehead and exploding from the top of their craniums, showering hair, flesh, and fluid every which way. He shifted, his hands held at waist height, the Colt barrels angled upwards, and fired twice.

The machine gunner, about to swing the .50 to slay the

Warrior, was hit in the face, a slug to each eye. His head
snapped back and he toppled over the tailgate.

With ambidextrous, lethal precision, and with a smile on
his lips, Hickok squeezed off round after round. His next
shot smashed the half-track's windshield, the driver stiffening
and slumping over the steering wheel, and without any
pressure on the brake, the half-track lurched ahead. Pre-
occupied with the gunman, the Hounds did not notice.

Blade did. He dropped, trying to remove Chastity from
the line of fire, and out of the corner of his right eye, as
he landed on his left side, he saw the half-track creep forward
and bump into one of the Hounds.

Five of the men in black were already down. Another
snapped off a shot from his rifle and received a slug in the
brain for his trouble.

Releasing Chastity, Blade swept his legs around, slamming
them into the Hound carrying his Bowies and upending the
man.

Hickok shot Captain Ludvin, the slug perforating the
officer's nostrils and flinging him to the grass.

Blade elbowed the Hound with the Bowies in the mouth,
dazing his foe, and yanked the Bowies from the Hound's
hand. Even as his palms caressed the hilts, Blade speared
them up and in, burying the keen blades in the Hound's
throat. He rolled onto his broad back, tugging the Bowies
out, assessing the situation in the blink of an eye.

Three of the squad were still standing. A man with a scar
on his chin elevated an M-16, but a slug in his right eye spun
him completely around and felled him in his tracks.

Leaving only two. Both were within six feet of Blade, one
to his left, the other his right. With the consummate skill
of someone who had practiced the technique countless times
over the years, Blade raised the knives overhead and threw
them. Their blades glistened in the sunlight as they flew into
the chests of their respective targets. Twelve inches of cold
steel were imbedded to the hilt in each Hound. Both men
looked astonished; both dropped their machine guns and

clutched at the Bowies; both gawked at Blade in amazement for a moment; and both sank into eternity without uttering a sound.

No sooner were the last of the squad dispatched than two more dangers loomed.

Blade, flat on his back, saw the massive wheels of the half-track coming at him, ten feet away.

"Blade!" Chastity shouted, lying four feet to the giant's left.

The Warrior threw himself to the left, grabbing the girl and rolling until he was certain he was well beyond the path of the armored vehicle. He rose to his knees in time to see Hickok, the Colts in their holsters, climb onto the cab of the half-track and clamber higher.

What the—!

A yell from the end of the field drew Blade's gaze, and there were over a dozen men in black charging toward the Warriors, the tall figure leading them.

Hickok leaped into the bed and stepped behind the big .50. He smirked as he swung the machine gun to cover the attacking Hounds. "Let's see how you coyotes like a taste of your own medicine," he said, and fired. The half-track was moving at a snail's pace, enabling him to aim with his customary deadly efficiency.

The .50-caliber made mincemeat of the Hounds, its heavy slugs ripping through the men in black and felling them in midstride. Geysers of blood spattered the grass as the thundering .50 mowed them down. Within 30 seconds all of the Hounds were dead except for two, the tall figure and one other. They had turned as the gunman began firing, and they managed to reach the protective shelter of the forest before the .50 bagged them.

His ears ringing, grinning impishly, Hickok peered over the smoking barrel at the row of crimson-dotted corpses. "Piece of cake," he said.

Blade rose, clutching Chastity in his left arm. He crossed to the nearest of the pair he'd slain with his Bowies and removed the knife. After wiping the blade clean on the Hound's black outfit, he repeated the procedure with the second commando.

The half-track continued to crawl toward the tree line.

"Daddy!" Chastity called excitedly.

"Don't yell," Blade advised, jogging after the vehicle.

"Why not?" Chastity inquired.

"If you make a lot of noise, you let your enemies know where you're at," Blade instructed her.

"Don't they already know where we're at?"

"Yes, but—"

"Then I don't see why I can't yell," Chastity declared.

"Because if you make a lot of noise, you draw their attention," Blade explained.

"But they're running away."

"I know, but—"

"Then why can't I yell?"

"Because I said so," Blade stated in a stern tone.

"Oh."

Blade looked at the half-track and observed the gunman swing into the cab from the roof. A moment later the vehicle clunked to a complete stop and the engine died.

"Isn't Daddy wonderful?" Chastity asked in awe.

"He has his moments," Blade admitted, grinning. He reached the driver's door and glanced up. "Are you okay?"

HIckok shoved the door wide and slid to the ground. "Fit as a fiddle." He took Chastity and squeezed her tight. "And how are you, princess?"

"Fine," Chastity answered. "But I was so scared for you."

"I was fakin'," Hickok detailed. "I wanted to catch these varmints by surprise, and my plan worked like a charm." He snickered, "We sure skunked them, didn't we?"

"Not quite," Blade said.

"How so?" Hickok responded.

"You're forgetting about Rikki."

Hickok gazed at the woods with a worried expression. "No, I'm not, pard."

CHAPTER FOUR

'Move it!'' General Thayer barked.

Rikki had heard the harsh sounds of the battle, anxiety flooding over him at the thought of his friends dying due to his negligence. He'd listened with baited breath when the gunfire abruptly stopped, and now the general and another man were racing up to the jeeps, both winded.

''What happened, sir?'' Sergeant Boynton asked.

General Thayer sat down in the passenger-side seat in the jeep Rikki occupied. ''I said move it!'' he snapped. The katana was snug under his belt on his right side.

''You heard the man,'' Boynton said to the four troopers, three of whom promptly climbed into the second jeep. The fourth took the wheel beside the general, while Boynton positioned himself at Rikki's side, hunching over and unslinging the HK-33.

''Memphis,'' General Thayer ordered the driver.

Rikki felt the jeep vibrate as the key was twisted in the ignition and the motor caught. The driver backed up, then took a sharp right, following a path of pulverized vegetation bearing the marks of caterpillar treads in the soft earth.

''If you don't mind my asking, sir,'' Sergeant Boynton ventured to inquire, ''where are the rest of the men?''

''Dead,'' General Thayer said angrily.

''All of them, sir?'' Boynton queried in astonishment.

"All of them," Thayer said.

"May I ask what happened?" Sergeant Boynton questioned.

"You may not."

"Sorry, sir."

General Thayer gazed speculatively at the martial artist. "Who *are* you?"

Rikki did not reply.

"I'll find out, sooner or later," General Thayer vowed. "One thing I do know. Whoever the hell the three of you are, you're damn good."

"The best," Rikki said.

"That leader of yours is unbelievable."

"Leader?" Rikki repeated quizzically. How did the general know Blade was the leader of the Warriors?

"Yeah. The guy in the buckskins. I've never seen anyone take such gambles," Thayer commented. "And fast! If I had a regiment like him, I'd conquer the whole continent."

The general was referring to Hickok! Rikki lowered his face so his captors couldn't see him grin.

"Something's nagging at me," General Thayer remarked. "There's something about the three of you, as if I should know you."

"We've never met before," Rikki said.

"I know." General Thayer scratched his chin. "Maybe it's something I've heard about you." He studied the small man, reflecting. "But what?"

"Sir," Sergeant Boynton interjected. "I've had the same feeling."

General Thayer glanced at the noncom. "You have?"

"Yes, sir. Ever since I saw this guy in action," Boynton said. "But I can't put my finger on it."

"This is most extraordinary," Thayer mentioned.

They drove in silence for the better part of 15 minutes, with the jeeps staying on the pathway of crushed vegetation until they came to a dirt road. There, they turned to the left.

"We'll be in Memphis in about a half-hour," General

Thayer said to the Warrior.

Rikki merely nodded.

"Provided we don't bump into a Leather Knight patrol, sir," Sergeant Boynton remarked.

"Use your head, Sergeant," General Thayer said. "The Leather Knights never send patrols southeast of the city, and you know it. St. Louis is northwest of Memphis, remember? That's why we encounter the Leather Knights on highways to the northwest."

"One day we'll wipe out those bastards," Sergeant Boynton declared. "Or should I say bitches, sir?"

General Thayer looked at his prisoner. "The Leather Knights are bikers, and their leaders are all women." He paused. "At least, they were all women once. But we've heard reports that some men are serving in leadership capacities now."

"I don't believe it, sir," Sergeant Boynton stated. "Those women would never allow a man to have a say in anything. They're all a bunch of rotten dykes."

"They are not," Rikki disputed him, and instantly regretted his impetuousness. But he would not permit an insult to his beloved Lexine to pass undefended. She had been a Leather Knight, until she'd tried to buck the system and been sentenced to death. He'd saved her, grown to love her, and taken her with him to the Home. The poignant memories of the run to St. Louis stirred his mind. He recalled, vividly, the battles with the Leather Knights; the repulsive rats; the savage mutants, Slither and Grotto; and the forging of an eternal binding amid the blazing heat of combat.

"You sound like you know the Leather Knights," General Thayer said suspiciously.

"The Knights are widely known," Rikki declared.

"One day we'll be as widely known as the Knights," Sergeant Boynton bragged to Rikki. "You wait and see."

The jeep unexpectedly arrived at an intersection with a paved highway. After braking and glancing both ways, the driver wheeled to the right. Marred, pitted, and warped by

105 years of abandoned neglect, the highway was in deplorable condition. The jeep bounced and bumped as it struck ruts and potholes.

"Where did you learn about the Leather Knights?" General Thayer inquired.

"Elsewhere," Rikki said.

"When?"

"A while ago."

"What do you know about them?"

Rikki shrugged. "This and that."

"Do you want me to slug him, sir?" Sergeant Boynton queried. "The son of a bitch needs to learn manners."

"In due course," General Thayer said patiently. He reached down and stroked the katana hilt. "We've never seen anyone with a fine sword like this. Perhaps the sword is the key. Perhaps . . ."

"What kind of sword is that, sir?" Boynton inquired.

"I don't . . ." General Thayer began, then snapped the fingers on his right hand. "That's it!"

"What, sir?" Sergeant Boynton asked.

"The outsider with the sword! Now I remember!" General Thayer exclaimed.

"I don't follow, sir."

General Thayer scrutinized their captive. "Yes. You *do* fit the description."

"Do I?" Rikki responded.

"What description, sir?" Sergeant Boynton inquired.

"Think back to the last Leather Knight patrol we ambushed," General Thayer said.

"I remember it, sir. I was there," Sergeant Boynton said.

"And we captured one of the Leather Knights, a man named Anson," General Thayer stated.

"The one we promised to spare if he provided information," Sergeant Boynton commented, and chuckled. "Of course, he was executed anyway."

"That's the one," General Thayer said. "He told us everything he knew about the Leather Knights. He even spun a tale about two outsiders who took on the Leather Knights and beat them on their own turf. I was positive he was concocting the story to prolong his life. Do you remember what he said?''

Sergeant Boynton recollected for several seconds. ''He claimed the outsiders killed dozens of Leather Knights, sir. One of them was supposed to be a giant armed with knives, and the other was a little guy with a sword!'' As he said the last words, his brown eyes narrowed, focused on the Warrior. ''You!''

''Yes, him,'' General Thayer confirmed.

Rikki stared at the trees alongside the road.

''Do you deny it was you?'' General Thayer asked the martial artist.

''Does it matter?'' Rikki responded.

''I told the King about the story,'' General Thayer said. ''He was very interested and wanted me to learn more about these outsiders. Two men holding their own against all the Knights seemed far-fetched at the time, but after seeing your friends and you in action, the idea isn't so crazy. If you are one of those outsiders, the King might strike a deal with you.''

''Like he did with the Leather Knight you executed?'' Rikki remarked.

''This is different,'' General Thayer said.

''I won't be as guillible as the Knight,'' Rikki assured him.

''I know you won't,'' Thayer agreed. ''And I won't make the mistake of underestimating you twice. If you are one of the outsiders the Knight talked about, then you were inside St. Louis. You know the layout. The knowledge you possess could be crucial to the success of our raid.''

''Raid?''

General Thayer nodded and grinned wickedly. ''The King has planned a raid on the Knights, an attack designed to eliminate their leadership in one swoop.''

''He has, sir?'' Sergeant Boynton asked eagerly.

''If you breathe one word of this, Sergeant, you or any

of your men, you will be summarily put to death," General Thayer warned.

"On my honor as a soldier, I won't," Sergeant Boynton promised. "None of these men will."

General Thayer shifted his attention back to the martial artist. "What's your name?"

Rikki maintained a stony profile.

"What harm can your name do?" the general demanded. "Make up one if you want. Just give me a name to use."

What harm *could* supplying his real name do? Rikki wondered. Plenty, he guessed, because the Leather Knights had known it. So his choices were clear. He could give them a false name, no name at all, or his real name and be willing to suffer the consequences. The words of his favorite book, the *I Ching*, served as a guidepost in this instance: "Words and deeds are the string and bow of the superior man. As the string and bow move, they accord honor or disgrace," he paraphrased aloud.

General Thayer and Sergeant Boynton exchanged perplexed looks. "What?" the general said.

"My name is Rikki-Tikki-Tavi."

"I knew it!" General Thayer declared.

"This *is* the guy, sir?" Boynton inquired.

"Is there any doubt?" General Thayer answered. "The King and the Dark Lord will both be pleased."

"Who is the Dark Lord?" Rikki inquired.

"The Dark Lord is the power behind the throne, so to speak," General Thayer said. "The King listens to no one but the Dark Lord."

"Have you seen this Dark Lord?" Rikki asked.

General Thayer nodded and licked his lips. "Yes. Once. The King escorted me into the Dark Lord's presence." He lowered his voice. "I never want to go through that again."

"You actually *saw* the Dark Lord?" Sergeant Boynton said, interrupting, so astounded by the revelation that he forgot military protocol.

The general, engrossed in a private terror, did not notice.

"I saw him. The King wanted to introduce me, his new commander in chief of the Hounds of Hades army."

"Then the King answers to one other?" Rikki probed, his curiosity stimulated.

"The King answers to the Dark Lord," Thayer divulged. "And the Dark Lord answers to no one."

"Is the Dark Lord a person or a mutant?" Rikki questioned.

"The Dark Lord is like nothing I've ever seen," General Thayer said. "And no one, other than me, has ever been in to see him and lived to talk about it."

"Is the Dark Lord male?" Rikki queried.

"I don't know."

"Now who's being evasive?" Rikki baited him.

"I honestly don't know," General Thayer said. "Maybe the Dark Lord is an 'it.' Whether the Dark Lord is male or female, or something in between, is irrelevant. The important thing to remember is that if the King takes you in to meet the Dark Lord, you'll never come out again."

The driver chose that moment to make an announcement. "The outskirts of Memphis, sir, dead ahead."

CHAPTER FIVE

"This is fun!"

"If you think this tin-plated rattletrap is something, wait until you take a gander at the buggy we have at our Home, princess," Hickok told her.

"You ride bugs?" Chastity asked in amazement.

"No," Blade answered with a laugh, his brawny hands on the steering wheel, his eyes glued to the trail of flattened vegetation the half-track was following. "Our Founder left us a special vehicle called the SEAL. It's solar powered and has amphibious capability."

"Amfibby-what?" Chastity said.

"The SEAL can travel on land or in the water," Blade explained. "We usually take the SEAL when we go on long runs, but not this time. A jet, a VTOL known as a Hurricane, flew us to Florida." He paused and frowned. "But the pilot never returned to pick us up."

"Good," Chastity stated.

"Good?" Blade responded.

"Yep. I wouldn't have my new daddy if you'd been picked up," Chastity noted.

"I never thought of it that way," Blade admitted.

"Out of the mouth of babes," Hickok quipped.

"I'm not a baby," Chastity said indignantly.

"I know, princess," Hickok said. "Just a figure of speech."

Chastity stared straight ahead, the wind ruffling her blonde locks. "I didn't know you could ride in these without a window."

"I had to remove the broken glass," Blade said. "But I wouldn't recommend driving like this on an extended trip."

"Why not?" Chastity asked.

"You wind up eating a lot of mosquitoes and flies," Blade detailed.

Chastity's forehead creased, her countenance betraying her confusion, until she abruptly cackled. "Oh! I get it!" She grimaced. "Yucko."

"Uh-oh," Hickok said.

Blade glanced at the gunman. "What is it?"

"Take a look-see," Hickok stated, nodding straight ahead.

Involved in his discussion with Chastity, Blade had given the track in front of them a cursory inspection. Now he scrutinized the terrain carefully and spied the reason for the gunfighter's concern. "An intersection," he muttered, applying the brakes and bringing the half-track to a halt at the junction with a dirt road.

"Which way do we go?" Chastity inquired.

"I wish I knew," Blade said, peeved. Yet another hindrance to locating Rikki! First, after Hickok had reloaded his Pythons, they had checked each body to insure all of the Hounds were dead. While thus engaged, they'd heard the sound of two or three vehicles hastening to the northwest. Blade had taken an Ingram M-10 from one of the corpses, along with six spare, full magazines. Each magazine held 30 rounds. He preferred the M-10 in this instance because of its compact size; even with the wire stock extended, the submachine gun was a mere 22 inches in length and weighed six and a half pounds.

At that point a decision had had to be made. Should they search in the forest for Rikki, or head out after the vehicles?

Blade had hoped for the latter recourse. His logic had been simple. The Hound captain, Ludvin, had claimed Rikki had been captured. And if the Hounds had caught the martial artist, then odds were those vehicles hauling butt to the northwest were transporting him.

At least, he'd hoped they were.

But now, after following the trail of flattened brush for nearly 15 minutes, he was beginning to entertain grave doubts.

What if he was wrong?

What if the captain had lied?

What if Rikki was lying back in the woods somewhere, injured, in desperate need of assistance?

"Which way do we go?" Chastity repeated, dispelling the giant's moody thoughts.

"Left," Blade said, and suited his next action to his words by hauling on the steering wheel and tromping on the gas.

"Why léft, pard?" Hickok inquired as the half-track performed the required turn.

"One of the Hounds mentioned Memphis," Blade said. "I suspect they're based there. If Rikki is their prisoner, then we'll find him in Memphis, and a left will take us in the direction of the city."

"If?" Hickok reiterated. "Didn't one of those lowlifes say Rikki is in their hands?"

"Yes," Blade confirmed.

"Then why so wishy-washy?"

"Must be my fatigue," Blade replied.

"We could all use ten hours of shut-eye," Hickok concurred.

"Why would you want to shut your eyes for ten hours?" Chastity inquired.

"Shut-eye is the same as sleep," Hickok informed her.

Chastity stared at the gunman for a moment. "Daddy?"

"Yeah, princess?"

"If I'm going to be your daughter, do I need to talk like

you do?''

"Of course not.''

"Whew! Thanks. For a minute there, I was really worried.''

They lapsed into silence as the half-track clattered along the dirt road, the afternoon heat climbing, the dust swirling in the shattered windshield, choking them, making them cough and stinging their eyes. Chastity rested with her head slumped on Hickok's arm.

Blade saw the next intersection before the others, and slowed. "Here we go again.''

Hickok, idly gazing at the landscape on the passenger side, straightened in his seat. "What is it, pard?'' he asked drowsily.

"Decision time,'' Blade declared, bringing the armored vehicle to a stop with its front bumper jutting into one lane of the paved highway.

"Which way?'' Hickok queried.

"If I'm correct about Memphis being northwest of here,'' Blade speculated, "then we take a right.''

"Go for it,'' Hickok prompted.

Blade did, shifting awkwardly, grinding the gears.

"I wish we could stash Chastity somewhere safe,'' Hickok remarked, looking at the cild's sleeping features fondly.

"When we reach Memphis, we can hide the half-track and leave her inside,'' Blade suggested.

"Not on your life.''

Blade detected a tine of apprehensiveness in the gunman's voice. "I'll be happy when we have her safely at the Home,'' he mentioned.

"You and me both,'' Hickok agreed. "It's sort of funny, isn't it?''

"What is?''

"All the places we've been to over the years, all the runs we've made, all the sights we've seen and the people we've met, and the one place where we're completely safe, the one spot in this whole blamed world where no one will try to blow us away, is at our Home with our Family,'' Hickok observed.

"And we're not even completely safe there,'' Blade pointed out. ''The Home has been attacked a number of times.''

''You know what I mean,'' Hickok said.

Blade nodded, and once more they fell quiet. He listened to the rumbling of the half-track motor, his senses dulled by the heat and his weariness. Daydreams of his wife and son, Jenny and Gabe, soothed his troubled mind. Lulled into complacency by the motion of the vehicle, he missed spotting the body until there was scarcely time to stop. As it was, as his drooping eyes spotted the prone figure lying across the center of the highway, he slammed on the brakes and yanked on the steering wheel, angling the half-track to the left. The brakes locked, and the vehicle slewed to a screeching halt within inches of the figure's head.

''What the heck!'' Hickok blurted, on the verge of dozing off himself.

''Daddy!'' Chastity cried, awakening abruptly and grabbing the gunman.

''Stay put,'' Blade directed, killing the motor and snatching the M-10 from the floor near his right boot. He pushed the door open and vaulted to the cracked asphalt. The body was on the passenger side, and he advanced cautiously around the front of the half-track, the M-10 leveled, his eyes raking the surrounding foliage.

Hickok's head popped through the windshield opening, his gaze swiveling to the roadway next to the front tire. ''Hey! There's a woman lyin' there.''

''I know,'' Blade said softly, stepping past the fender and seeing her clearly.

''What'd you do? Run over her?''

''Be serious.''

''I am,'' Hickok asserted. ''I've seen the way you drive

sometimes.'' The Pythons materialized in his hands. ''I'll cover you.'' He watched the highway alertly.

Blade knelt slowly, reaching out with his left hand and grasping her right shoulder. He started to roll her over.

With surprising swiftness, the woman completed the roll on her own, a Caspian Arms Commander 45 in her right hand. She pressed the barrel against the Warrior's chin. ''Don't move!''

Blade was able to take in her long brunette hair, her piercing hazel eyes, and her rounded cheeks and pointed chin before she hissed the warning again. ''Don't move, sucker!'' A ragged green shirt, torn jeans, and faded brown boots clothed her lithe frame. He wagged the M-10, which was pointed at her abdomen.

''Drop it!'' she snapped.

''I think we have a tie here,'' Blade said calmly.

''Tie, hell. You drop it or I'll put a hole in you the size of my fist,'' the woman threatened.

''What the blazes is going on down there?'' Hickok called out.

''You! In the cab!'' the woman yelled.

''Who are you?'' Hickok responded, glancing down. His view of the woman was obstructed by Blade's massive form.

''Never mind. Throw your weapons out or I'll shoot your friend,'' she declared.

''Blade, did you get caught again?'' Hickok asked.

''So it would seem,'' Blade responded in a low tone to avoid agitating the woman.

''Pitiful. Just pitiful. Are you tryin' to set the new world record for the most times being captured in one day?'' Hickok queried.

''You have no room to talk,'' Blade commented.

The woman's eyes widened in astonishment. ''Are you crazy? I have a gun on you! I could kill you.''

''If you'd wanted to kill me, I'd already be dead,'' Blade said.

''Drop your machine gun,'' she insisted.

"No," Blade replied.

"I don't believe this," the woman stated angrily. "This is not the way it's supposed to work."

"Why don't we discuss this intelligently?" Blade proposed.

"Drop your damn gun or I'll shoot you!" she vowed, her facial muscles tightening.

"No, you won't," Blade said.

"And why won't I?" she demanded.

"Because if you do, ma'am," interjected a voice next to her head, "I'm afraid I'll be obligated to ventilate your noggin."

Startled, she looked up to discover a smiling blond man in buckskins with a pair of gleaming revolvers trained on her forehead. "Where'd you come from?" she blurted.

The blond man's smile widened. "I'm an expert at tippy-toe."

"You *are* crazy!" she exclaimed. "Both of you."

"*We're* crazy?" Hickok responded. "You're the one tryin' to bushwhack a half-track, for cryin' out loud."

"We need this!" she said.

"We?" Blade repeated.

"Don't move!" commanded a man to their rear, the effect of his command vitiated by the quavering manner in which it was delivered.

Blade glanced over his left shoulder. "Oh, boy."

"What is it now?" Hickok inquired, his Pythons fixed on the woman.

"You won't believe me," Blade said.

"I'll believe you," Hickok promised.

"There's a guy covering us with a bazooka."

"I don't believe it," Hickok said, and risked a quick look behind them.

A thin, short man in a soiled brown suit, wire-rimmed glasses perched on the tip of his nose, stood 30 feet away. Cradled on his right shoulder was a bazooka.

"Now we've got you!" the woman gloated. "Make one

false move and Clyde will blow you to smithereens.''

"Clyde?" Hickok said.

"That's right!" Clyde chimed in. "One move and you're history."

Blade straightened. "You won't fire."

"Why won't I?" Clyde demanded.

"This must be amateur hour," Hickok muttered, then impatiently yelled at the man in the brown suit. "You won't fire, you ninny, because if you do, you'll hit this dingbat too."

"Who are you calling a dingbat?" the woman asked.

Clyde appeared to be mulling over the situation, and he grinned as an idea occurred to him. "I've got it! You two stand still while Bonnie moves aside. Then I can blow you to smithereens."

"I'm dreaming all of this," Hickok said to Blade. "Tell me I'm dreaming all of this."

"Drop your bazooka," Blade instructed the aspiring ambusher, "or we'll shoot the woman."

"You wouldn't dare!" the woman responded defiantly.

"Don't shoot Bonnie," Clyde said.

"Then drop the blamed bazooka!" Hickok snapped. "We don't have the time for this nonsense. Drop it, now, or I'll plug the ding-a-ling."

"Do you mean me?" Bonnie queried.

"Do you see any other ding-a-lings around here?" Hickok answered. Then he gazed at Clyde. "Other than Bozo, of course."

Bonnie's lower lips began to tremble and her cheeks turned red. "You're—you're—" she sputtered, then finally finished the sentence. "Rude!"

Hickok glanced at Blade. "Would you sock me on the jaw?"

"Why?"

"I'd like to wake up now," Hickok declared.

Blade stared at the man with the bazooka. "I won't say it again. Drop it!"

''Don't listen!'' Bonnie urged. ''We can take these jerks.''

''You and what ten armies?'' Hickok retorted.

''Oh, yeah?'' Bonnie rejoined. ''So you think we're amateurs, do you? I'll show you!'' And with that, she pressed the Caspian into the giant's groin and squeezed the trigger.

CHAPTER SIX

Memphis was a typical post-apocalypse metropolis, a wrecked relic of a bygone era, some areas a shadowy shambles, other areas partially, crudely restored. Like many an American city, Memphis had been spared a direct nuclear strike. World War Three had not resulted in the ultimate Armageddon everyone feared. Neither side wanted to thoroughly annihilate the other; conquest was the goal, and conquest implied having something worth conquering after the last missile was launched and the decisive bomb dropped. The American public, conditioned to near-mass hysteria by an alarmist, self-aggrandizing media and headline-seeking politicians, expected the world to wither and die, totally ignoring the lessons to be learned from Hiroshima and Nagasaki. Within 40 years of World War Two, within four decades of the date the first atomic bomb was used on major cities, both seaports were inhabited by predominantly healthy citizens and could boast gardens the equal of any others on the planet.

The aftermath of World War Three was no different. Cities like New York and San Diego, struck by large-megaton weapons, were reduced to molten slag. But municipalities such as Memphis, lacking any primary military significance, were seldom hit. In military circles, Memphis was rated as a secondary target, not worthy of being hit in the first strike, and consequently slated for one of the follow-up bomber or missile attacks. Fortunately for Memphis, the war was over before the Soviets could get around to destroying it.

All of these recollections filtered through Rikki-Tikki-Tavi's mind as the two jeeps traveled into the heart of the city. Most of the buildings were vacant and dilapidated. Rikki speculated that the populace had been evacuated once, for whatever reason, and had never returned. He knew the government had forcibly transported people from the Eastern cities to the Midwest. Perhaps the population of Memphis was one of those forced to relocate. Since then, the city had literally gone to the dogs.

Packs of canines roamed the streets seeking rats and other small game. Piles of refuse littered the sidewalks. Looters had wrecked all the business establishments, and the residential neighborhoods were in an advanced stage of disrepair. Overall, Memphis reeked, a subtle, putrid odor permeating the oppressive atmosphere. The dogs were in their element, scouring the buildings and alleys for meals and functioning as a collective early-warning system for the other inhabitants of Memphis.

The humans.

Occupying decayed, ramshackle structures in the center of Memphis, the human element was a motley collection of scavengers, outlaws, and outcasts. Except for the Hounds, whose neat black uniforms lent them the distinction of seeming to be from a higher, advanced civilization, the people of Memphis were attired in grubby clothes only a degree cleaner than themselves.

Rikki memorized the sequence of highways and streets the jeeps traversed for future use. They entered Memphis on U.S. Highway 78, which became Lamar Avenue, and eventually turned south on Airways Boulevard. The next turn, on Ball Road, was to the west.

"Our Headquarters Complex," General Thayer said, indicating a fenced area adjacent to Ball Road to the north.

Rikki noticed a bustle of activity on the far side of the

fence. Men in black were drilling in a parking lot, marching and exercising and practicing hand-to-hand combat. Others were loading equipment and supplies into a parked convoy of eight trucks. Rikki abruptly realized he'd seen only four battered cars and one pickup the whole trip. "Did you construct your headquarters?" he idly asked.

"We repaired this installation," Thayer said. "This facility was the Memphis Defense Depot before the war, and it was a junky dump when we took it over. The King wanted us to have our headquarters located near his mansion, and this was convenient. Took us months to fix the site up."

"The King isn't here?"

General Thayer laughed. "The King is at his mansion. He wouldn't live in a barracks with two dozen grunts."

"When will I meet him?"

"What's your rush, pal?" General Thayer responded. "After I detail a platoon to go back and nab your buddies, we'll be heading for the King's mansion."

"Is such a plan wise?" Rikki inquired.

"What do you mean?"

"Can you afford to lose more men?" Rikki elaborated.

"Smart ass," General Thayer mumbled. He chewed on his lower lip nervously.

Rikki noted the officer's reaction. "I understand that you trained the Hounds," he remarked.

"Yes," General Thayer said proudly. "I whipped a no-talent bunch of misfits into a top-notch fighting outfit."

"Your men did display outstanding discipline when they attempted to subdue me," Rikki conceded.

General Thayer was genuinely flattered. "Thank you. Coming from a man of your caliber, that's quite a compliment."

"And where did you acquire your expertise?" Rikki asked tactfully.

In the twinkling of an eye, the officer's expression changed drastically. He frowned and averted his eyes.

"The general's past is a sensitive subject," Sergeant Boynton said. "One better left alone."

"I can speak for myself, Sergeant," General Thayer stated.

"Sorry, sir."

Thayer cleared his throat and looked at the martial artist. "My prior experience was acquired in Sparta."

Rikki's brow creased. "Sparta?"

"You've never heard of it?" General Thayer asked.

"We studied the history of Greece in our school," Rikki said. "We learned about Sparta, Athens, and the rest of the Greek city-states. Sparta was renowned for her military prowess and for the quality of her soldiers. The Spartans and the Japanese samurai were the two greatest warrior castes the world has ever seen."

"Again you impress me," General Thayer declared. "But I wasn't referring to the Spartans of antiquity. Another Sparta has arisen."

Rikki's surprise showed.

"I was born in Sparta," General Thayer went on without noticing. "I spent thirty years of my life there, and I was trained by Spartan instructors. There are none finer."

"Where is this new Sparta located?" Rikki queried.

"I'm not at liberty to say."

"I'd like to hear about it," Rikki said, hoping to coax the information from the officer. Another Sparta! If the new one was anything like the ancient Sparta, the Family Elders would be intensely interested in ascertaining Sparta's location. And the Freedom Federation would welcome another ally.

"I can't say," General Thayer snapped. "I won't say. I pledged never to reveal Sparta's location, and it's a promise I'll never break."

"Why did you leave?"

"I didn't leave," Thayer said, downcast. "I was booted out."

Rikki was an astute judge of human nature, and he

perceived an incongruity in the general's behavior. The Spartans expelled the man, yet he held them in the highest regard. Why? He waited for Thayer to elaborate, but the general changed the subject.

"So I drifted like a common scavenger until I reached Memphis," Thayer detailed. "The King was in the process of organizing his campaign. Boynton and a few others were already with him. He saw fit to honor me with command, and I haven't disappointed him."

The jeeps were slowing as they neared a gate.

"What is the King's campaign?" Rikki probed.

"Ask him when you meet him," General Thayer said.

A pair of men in black, both with slung AR-15's, stood guard at the closed gate. They saluted the general as his jeep braked, then hurried to swing the gate inward.

"I haven't noticed any female Hounds," Rikki commented.

"And you won't," General Thayer said. "The King doesn't want women in his army. He claims women are inferior fighters."

"He is mistaken," Rikki said. "I have close friends, female Warriors, who are the equal of any man."

"You know he's wrong, and I know he's wrong, but I'm not about to commit suicide by telling the King to his face," General Thayer declared. The jeep drove into the complex.

"He would kill you?"

"In a minute, if killing me suited his purpose," Thayer said. "But he won't because I'm valuable to him. I've created a crack tactical unit he can employ to further his ambition. He has the grand schemes, and I put them into effect."

"Why do you work for him if he is so unstable?" Rikki asked.

The former Spartan gazed thoughtfully at the martial artist. "I've asked myself the same thing time and again." He sighed. "I guess I'm trying to prove something to myself, to prove I'm competent at my trade. Besides, I have nowhere else to go. Memphis is as good as anywhere else."

"So you work for a man who is mentally unbalanced," Rikki remarked.

"I never said that," General Thayer responded testily. "And quit trying to put words in my mouth. It won't work."

"What?"

"Don't play innocent with me," Thayer declared. "You're trying to turn me against the King. Well, you're wasting your time. For better or worse, I'm with the King for the duration."

The jeeps braked in front of a large structure fabricated from corrugated metal and painted green.

"This is my Command Center," General Thayer disclosed. "You will stay in the jeep while I attend to dispatching a platoon." He looked at the noncom. "Watch him closely, Sergeant."

"Yes, sir."

The officer entered the Command Center.

"I like him a lot," Sergeant Boynton mentioned.

"Do you like the King too?" Rikki inquired.

Boynton shrugged. "I'm not being paid to like the King, just to kick ass for him. And I like kicking ass."

"The King pays you?"

"Did you think we're all in this for our health?" Sergeant Boynton rejoined. "Except for the general, the rest of us are in this for the gold."

"Gold?"

"The King has a hoard of gold in his mansion," Boynton said. "A room full of the stuff. Gold, mister, is the one commodity you can exchange everywhere. Gold talks. It's not like the old paper money, which isn't worth the paper it was printed on. Oh, I hear that a few places will honor the paper junk, but only because they can't print their own— and even then they back the paper crap with gold or silver." He smiled. "Gold can get a person anything they want."

"Then you did not tell the truth earlier," Rikki observed.

"What are you talking about?"

"You told me that you're not a professional mercenary,"

Rikki said, "but you are. You fight for money."

"Only until I've saved enough gold."

"How much is enough?" Rikki asked.

"Until I'm satisfied," Boynton said.

"You'll never be satisfied."

"You think so?"

"I know so," Rikki stated. "True satisfaction comes from living a life devoted to spiritual truth, not collecting material wealth. You'll never be satisfied because you'll always want more."

Sergeant Boynton snickered. "Wait until I tell the general you're a religious fanatic."

"Are you religious?"

"Me? Hell, no!" Boynton chuckled. "Religion is mumbo jumbo. There's no God."

General Thayer stepped from the Command Center and crossed to the jeep. "Let's go," he said to the driver as he climbed in. "We're taking our prisoner to the King."

"Here's a laugh for you, sir," Sergeant Boynton said. "This guy is religious."

Thayer glanced at the Warrior. "You are? Then you'd better start praying to whatever deity you worship. You're going to need all the help you can get."

CHAPTER SEVEN

Blade felt goose bumps prick his skin as the Caspian barrel poked into his genitals. In the instant before she squeezed the trigger, instinctively, fleetingly terrified at the prospect of losing his organ, he involuntarily flinched, his breath catching in his throat.

But nothing happened.

The gun didn't fire.

"What the hell!" Bonnie exclaimed, lowering the Caspian and gazing at the firearm in disbelief. "I loaded it myself!" Her astonishment over the auto pistol's presumed failure to discharge was abruptly changed to fear for her personal safety when the giant clamped his left hand on the front of her green shirt and hauled her into the air.

"Put her down!" Clyde shouted, running toward them, the bazooka flapping on his shoulder.

"Put me down, you big ox!" Bonnie shrieked, kicking and thrashing.

"Let me sock her on the jaw?" Hickok asked.

Blade pressed the M-10 up to Bonnie's mouth. "Drop the damn gun, *Now!*"

Frightened by the fury on his features, Bonnie released the Caspian and ceased struggling.

"Let go of her!" yelled Clyde, still 15 feet off.

"How about lettin' me sock *him* on the jaw?" Hickok

requested.

Ignoring the gunfighter's cracks, Blade dumped Bonnie onto the asphalt. "Don't move," he growled.

"I'd like to sock somebody in the jaw," Hickok mumbled.

Clyde pounded to within four feet of the Warriors and pointed the bazooka at Blade. "Run, Bonnie! I'll protect you."

Annoyed to the limits of his endurance, Blade glared at the bespectacled bantamweight, then glanced at Hickok. "Him!" he ordered.

Grinning in delight, the gunman twirled the Pythons into their holsters, the sunlight glinting from the steel.

Distracted by the spinning revolvers, Clyde shifted his gaze from the giant to the gunman. As he did, he accidentally tilted the bazooka upward and fired. A thunderous blast accompanied the launching of the finned rocket and hot gases were expelled out the rear of the smooth-bore tube, scorching the ground behind him. Clyde fell onto his posterior.

Five pairs of eyes gaped at the rocket's trajectory as the projectile arced skyward, then descended in a graceful loop and struck the earth 300 yards distant, disappearing in the forest on the right side of the highway. The explosion sent shredded leaves, bits of bark, dirt, weeds, and the feathers from a roosting flock of starlings swirling into the atmosphere.

Blade smacked his left palm against his forehead and closed his eyes.

"You idiot!" Bonnie snapped at her defender.

Clyde appeared on the verge of tears.

His right fist clenched in preparation for delivering a blow to Clyde's jaw, Hickok watched three injured starlings striving to become airborne. "Wow. I'd like to take this guy fishin' sometime," he quipped.

"Yippee!" enthused an unexpected spectator, applauding. "Do that again!"

Everyone glanced at the half-track.

"How did you do that?" Chastity asked. She was sitting

on the hood next to the windshield, her wondering gaze on the bazooka.

"What are you doing up there?" Hickok demanded.

"Watching the fireworks," Chastity answered. "We had fireworks in Atlanta once a year on Civil Rights day."

"How did you get on the hood?" Hickok inquired.

"I crawled through the window," Chastity said, gesturing at the missing windshield.

"Get down from there," Hickok directed, stepping close to the fender and extending his arms. "I'll catch you."

Giggling, Chastity slid down the hood into his waiting hands. "Who is the pretty lady?" she inquired.

Bonnie was staring at the girl in transparent bewilderment. "You have a child with you!" she blurted.

"What was your first clue?" Hickok responded.

Her eyes widening, Bonnie studied the gunman and the giant. "Hey! Where are your uniforms?"

"We don't wear uniforms," Blade said.

"But Hounds always wear black uniforms," Bonnie reiterated.

"We're not Hounds, dingbat," Hickok stated.

"Not Hounds?" Bonnie shook her head and gazed at her companion. "They're not Hounds!"

"Apparently we committed a slight blunder," Clyde said.

"You boneheaded cow chip! You could've killed us," Hickok snapped.

"We thought you were Hounds," Bonnie declared.

"If we'd been Hounds, you'd both be dead," Blade informed her. He leaned over and snatched the Caspian from the roadway. "The two of you should seriously consider another line of work."

"This isn't our vocation," Clyde said, and giggled.

Blade tucked the M-10 under his left arm and proceeded to inspect the Commander. "Have you ever shot one of these before?" he asked Bonnie.

"No," she admitted.

"Thank the Spirit," Blade remarked, glancing at Hickok.

"I'll be able to have more children because she didn't know a round has to be fed into the chamber before the gun will fire."

"Let's hear it for stupidity," the gunman joked.

"Who are you calling stupid?" Bonnie retorted.

"If the shoe fits . . ." Hickok said.

"I want some answers," Blade announced, squatting and looking from Bonnie to Clyde and back again. "Why did you jump the half-track? What were you trying to accomplish?"

"Don't tell him a thing," Clyde stated. "He could be working for the King."

"We're not," Blade said. "We've never even met this King."

"Then why are you driving the Hounds' half-track?" Clyde demanded.

"We stole it from them," Blade replied. "We're after the Hounds. They've taken a friend prisoner."

"You can kiss him good-bye," Bonnie remarked.

"Not on your life," Hickok vowed. "Warriors never desert their pards. And if the Hounds hurt our sidekick, I won't leave a Hound alive."

"I'm still not convinced we can trust you," Clyde commented.

Hickok deposited Chastity on the ground. "Is that a fact?" he said, then drew his right Colt ever so slowly. He cocked the hammer, took a stride, and touched the barrel to the tip of Clyde's nose. "I don't much care whether you trust us or not."

"You won't shoot," Clyde blustered.

The gunman leaned forward, smiling. "Look into my eyes," he directed.

Clyde obeyed.

"I'll count to three. If you haven't started spillin' the beans by the time I get to three, I'll plug you," Hickok said.

"You're bluffing," Clyde declared.

"One," Hickok stated.

"You wouldn't dare," Clyde maintained.

"Don't mess with him, Clyde," Bonnie urged nervously.

"Don't look," Blade said to Chastity.

"Two," Hickok continued.

Clyde licked his lips and glanced at Bonnie. "I think he means it."

"Then tell them!" Bonnie prompted.

"Adios," Hickok said, gouging the Python into Clyde's nostrils. "Get set to greet your Maker."

"No!" Clyde cried. "Don't! I'll talk! What do you want to know?" His glasses were tilted at an angle.

Hickok lowered the Colt. "I want you to answer every question the Big Guy asks. If you don't . . ." He wagged the Colt for emphasis, then twirled the Python into its holster.

"Now then," Blade said, "let's start at the beginning. My name is Blade. This is Hickok and his daughter, Chastity. A friend of ours by the name of Rikki-Tikki-Tavi has been captured by the Hounds. What do you know about them?"

Bonnie uttered a snorting noise. "What *don't* we know?"

"Are they based in Memphis?" Blade inquired.

"Yes," Bonnie confirmed. "Their Headquarters Complex is in the center of the city." She paused. "The bastards."

"You don't like them?"

"I hate the sons—" Bonnie began to respond, but amended her statement after glancing at Chastity. "The scum."

"Why?"

"Two reasons. First, they wouldn't let Clyde join the Hounds. They claimed he wasn't fit enough, but Boynton rigged his entrance test."

"Explain," Blade said.

"Boynton has had the hots for me for two years," Bonnie disclosed. "Ever since my brother and I came to Memphis."

"Clyde is your brother?" Blade deduced.

"Yep," Bonnie verified. "And he wants to join the Hounds. Sergeant Boyndon is in charge of giving the entrance tests for each candidate, and he deliberately fixed the test so Clyde would fail."

"Boynton told me to do one hundred push-ups," Clyde interrupted. "Nobody can do one hundred push-ups."

"I can," Blade said.

"That's not the point," Bonnie declared. "No one has ever had to do one hundred push-ups to get into the Hounds. Boynton made the test impossible for Clyde to pass because I won't go to bed with him."

"What does all of this have to do with ambushing the half-track?" Blade probed.

"We're leaving Memphis. And before we go, we want to pay the sons—scum—back for what they did. No one humiliates us and gets away with it," Bonnie affirmed.

"But ambush a half-track?" Blade queried in disbelief.

"Why do you think we swiped the bazooka from the Hound armory? I distracted the guard last night while Clyde snuck in and took the bazooka. We know how much the half-track means to the King and the Hounds."

"So to teach the Hounds a lesson, you planned to destroy the half-track?" Blade said.

"You got it." Bonnie laughed. "It was my idea."

"I couldn't talk her out of it," Clyde mentioned. "She's always doing something rash." He sighed. "I wanted to forget the whole affair, but she insisted on getting even. She can't stand being insulted, and she has a temper you wouldn't believe."

"I'd believe it," Hickok interjected.

"Early last night she dragged me off to the rear fence of the Hound Headquarters Complex," Clyde detailed. "The armory is situated at the back of the complex. She kept the gate guard busy, and I climbed over the fence and took the bazooka. I was surprised at how easy it was. They didn't even have the door locked—I guess because no one has ever attacked Memphis or tried to sneak into their complex. No one would be crazy enough to try."

"How did you keep the guard busy?" Hickok asked.

Bonnie smiled seductively and winked. "Use your imagination. Jeff and I were together for a while about ten months ago, and I found out he'd be on duty last night. He was putty in my hands, if you get my drift."

"I don't," Chastity said.

"You're not supposed to," Hickok declared.

Blade rose, wedged the Caspian under his belt, and gripped the M-10 in his right hand. He stared at the brother, then the sister. "You're free to go."

"You're not going to kill us?" Bonnie asked.

"Not unless you press the issue," Blade replied wryly. "You can take off." He gazed at the bazooka, on the asphalt alongside Clyde. "Do you have any more rockets?"

"Yes," Clyde answered. "The bazooka was packed in a small crate with six rockets. Thankfully, there was an instruction booklet."

"Where's the crate?"

"In the trees," Clyde said, motioning at the forest on the left.

"Go get it," Blade commanded. "We'll need it more than you."

Clyde went to stand.

"Hold it, dummy," Bonnie stated, heaving erect and facing the giant. "We'll give it to you on one condition."

"What condition?"

"That you take us with you," Bonnie said.

"Forget it."

"What's wrong with the idea?" Bonnie demanded. "You can use our help. There are too many Hounds for the two of you to take on by yourselves."

Blade studied the woman for several seconds. "Why would you want to help us?"

"That's my business," Bonnie said. "What do you say? We know Memphis inside and out. We can get you to the heart of the city without being spotted by the Hounds. We're your best bet to get your friend out alive."

"I don't like this idea, sis," Clyde remarked.

Bonnie looked at him. "You don't have to go. I'll understand. I know how your eyes are."

"What about your eyes?" Blade queried.

Clyde tapped his silver, wire-rimmed glasses. "I must wear corrective lenses. For years Bonnie had to lead me around by the hand, until we stumbled across this old optometry shop. There were dozens of glasses in a partially collapsed room. I tried on every one. These correct my vision adequately if I keep them on the end of my nose." He paused. "You're not leaving me behind, Bonnie."

"You don't need to come," she said.

"I'm coming along, and that's that."

"Both of you can join us," Blade commented. "But first, I want the crate."

"We'll go get it," Bonnie said, walking toward the trees. 'Our suitcase too, if you don't mind."

"Bring it," Blade responded. He watched them hurry into the woods.

"What gives, pard?" Hickok inquired.

"We can use their assistance. They know Memphis. We don't. It's as simple as that."

"Bull manure. Don't tell me you're buyin' the story about the entrance test?" the gunman asked.

"I believe they were telling the truth, as far as they went," Blade said. "But there's more here than meets the eye."

"Any clues?"

Blade shrugged. "Time will tell."

"I'll keep my eyes on them, just in case," Hickok promised.

"And I'll keep my eyes on you, Daddy," Chastity chimed in.

"I feel safer already."

CHAPTER EIGHT

The King certainly lived in a style consistent with his title. The mansion was huge and immaculately preserved, with a recent coat of white paint and all of its windows intact. Four large marble columns fronted a neatly trimmed green lawn. Access to the estate was through an arched silver gate guarded by ten men in black. A drive curved from the gate to the mansion and looped back again. Flower beds adorned the lawn; hickory trees afforded shade from the summer sun; and robins and mockingbirds foraged for worms.

Rikki glanced overhead at a sign attached to the top of the gate as the general's jeep drove past the saluting guards. The sign read "Destiny."

"The King believes in destiny," General Thayer explained, noticing the martial artist's gaze. "Specifically, his destiny. He believes he was born to rule."

"Do you think the Dark Lord is watching us right this minute, sir?" Sergeant Boynton asked anxiously.

General Thayer scrutinized the windows. Heavy drapes obscured the interiors of most of the rooms. "I wouldn't be surprised."

"Damn! This place gives me the creeps. Sir."

"Would you like to know a secret, Sergeant?" Thayer responded.

"Yes, sir."

"This place gives me the creeps too," General Thayer confessed.

Rikki saw six more Hounds on the steps leading to the entrance, all standing at attention. He mentally suppressed all nervousness over his impending encounter with the King, emptying himself of all emotion so he could function with all of his senses at their sharpest. The perfected swordsmaster must be ready to seize the advantage at any given moment. All of his faculties must be focused on the here and now.

"For what it's worth," General Thayer said, "I hope the King doesn't kill you. Another time, under different circumstances, we might have been friends." He smiled. "Pip-squeak."

The jeep cruised to a smooth stop at the base of the steps.

"Allow me," Thayer stated, producing a set of keys from his left front pant pocket and unfastening the cuffs binding the Warrior's ankles.

"What about the wrists?" Rikki asked, offering his arms.

General Thayer pocketed the keys. "Sorry. Let's go." He climbed from the jeep and waited for Rikki and Sergeant Boynton to join him. The noncom appeared slightly pale.

One of the Hounds on guard duty, standing to the right of the wooden door at the top of the steps, saluted. "The King is expecting you, sir," he announced.

Squaring his shoulders, the general headed for the door.

Rikki-Tikki-Tavi followed slowly, his legs tingling as his circulation was restored. He tensed and relaxed his thigh muscles repeatedly as he climbed the steps, wanting to restore mobility as quickly as possible. His wrists ached, but the flexibility in his arms had not been affected by the lengthy, cramped ride.

The Hound at the top opened the door and stood aside.

General Thayer rested his right hand on the hilt of the katana and walked into the mansion.

Surreptitiously testing the strength of the links securing his wrists, Rikki stayed on the general's heels.

Sergeant Boynton brought up the rear.

Rikki's first impression was of a profound quietude. The moment Boynton closed the door, all sound ceased. Dim illumination was furnished by small bulbs spaced at ten-foot intervals in the hall ceiling. The inside of the mansion was at least five degrees cooler than the outside temperature, contributing to the palpable aura of evil the mansion radiated. He stared at the nearest light. "Does the King have a generator?"

"Two," General Thayer replied. "The only working pair in Memphis. One is always on standby in case the primary fails."

Rikki surveyed his surroundings. The spacious central hallway ran the width of the mansion. Beautiful paintings, some of landscapes, some of diverse human subjects, and others obviously abstracts, lined the white walls. To the right a wide stairway curved upward to the next floor. Plush blue carpet was underfoot.

"We go up the stairs," General Thayer said, leading the way.

"Who owned this mansion before the King?" Rikki asked.

"No one," Thayer answered. "The estate was overgrown with weeds and the house was a mess. No one lived here for decades. There's a rumor, although I don't know how true it is, that a real king lived here before the war."

"America didn't have a royal family," Rikki said.

"Maybe it was a king from another country," General Thayer speculated with a shrug. "I don't know." He gazed at the polished gold bannister. "Whoever the hell lived here was a rich mother, I can tell you that. Most of what you see was already here when the King moved in. The rest was scrounged by the Hounds on raids."

Rikki stared at a life-sized portrait dominating the next landing. The man depicted was endowed with an innate dignity the artist had faithfully captured on canvas: brooding, yet sensitive eyes; black hair coiffured in an oiled pompadour, with bushy sideburns framing the ears; and exceedingly handsome features reflecting an inherent sensuality. The man wore black leather clothing, enhancing his virile image. "The mansion had not been ransacked?" Rikki asked in surprise.

"Nope," General Thayer responded. "Weird, isn't it? Every building in Memphis was looted except this one."

"Why?" Rikki wondered.

"I don't know," Thayer said. "Maybe the people considered this place special." He nodded at the painting. "There are several of him in the mansion. I guess he must have been the owner. Perhaps he was revered by the people, or they were afraid of him. But for whatever reason, the mansion wasn't touched."

"There could be another reason, sir," Sergeant Boynton whispered.

"What, Sergeant?"

"The Dark Lord. No one in their right mind would want to come near him. Or it," Sergeant Boynton theorized.

"Could be," General Thayer said. "But I doubt it. There were no reports of the Dark Lord until after the King moved into the mansion."

Rikki's interest was stimulated. "Really?"

General Thayer nodded. They reached the landing. "The Dark Lord's first victim was killed on this very floor."

"What happened?" Rikki queried.

The general took a right and strolled along another opulently decorated corridor. "The King had been in the mansion about a month. There was a captain in the Hounds, a man by the name of Lewis, who began grumbling about the arrangement. He wasn't satisfied living at the Headquarters Complex, which we were rebuilding at the time, and he groused to everyone who would listen about the King living in luxury while the rest of the men slept on cots."

"Lewis should have left well enough alone, sir," Sergeant Boynton said softly.

"But he didn't, despite my warnings," General Thayer stated. They passed a closed door on the right. "One day the King called a conference for all of his officers in his throne room.''

"He has a throne room?" Rikki repeated.

Thayer nodded. "You'll be there in a minute. Anyway, the King called this meeting for his general staff. He singled out Lewis. Told Lewis that if he wasn't satisfied with the status quo, then Lewis should file a formal complaint with the Dark Lord. That was the first any of us ever heard the name. Lewis, the fool, took the King up on the offer. So the King escorted Lewis into the Dark Lord's chamber.'' He paused, licking his lips.

"And then what?" Rikki probed.

"We all heard this terrible roar,'' General Thayer responded, his words barely audible. "The most awful sound you can imagine. Screeching and wailing like you wouldn't believe, and it went on and on and on. When the noise stopped, the King came out, and he was carrying Lewis.''

"Was Lewis dead?" Rikki asked.

"As a doornail," General Thayer answered. "The King ordered us to dispose of the body.'' He halted and looked at the Warrior. "And do you want to hear the strange part? We couldn't find a mark on Lewis. We stripped him and searched him from head to toe, and there wasn't so much as a scratch. Yet there he was, dead.'' He gazed at the floor, frowning. "That was just the beginning. Since then, the Dark Lord has claimed over two dozen victims.''

"Were they all killed in the mansion?''

"No. Most were, but seven or eight were mysteriously disposed of outside the estate. The majority of those killed were Hounds who committed a breach of discipline and were on report. A few were ordinary riffraff. One was a wandering bum. And no one was ever able to find a mark on any of them. They simply keeled over and died.''

"There must be a cause," Rikki said.

"I've tried to discover it, but couldn't,'' General Thayer declared. He glanced up at Rikki. "No one knows when their time will come, and the Dark Lord can strike anywhere. We've found victims in locked rooms at the HQ. Once, a Hound went AWOL, and we found his body ten miles from Memphis, slumped in the jeep he'd stolen.'' He swallowed hard. ''It's enough to give a person nightmares.''

And suddenly Rikki discerned the motivation behind Thayer's character. The man lived in fear of the Dark Lord. Was fear, then, the basis for the Spartan's misguided devotion to the King? Was Thayer deluding himself? Did the fear indicate the reason for Thayer's expulsion from Sparta? Or was Thayer trying to prove something to himself by working for the King—possibly attempting to prove he could conquer fear?

The general resumed walking down the corridor.

''Does the King have a mate?'' Rikki casually inquired.

Thayer snickered. ''I told you how the King feels about women. He thinks they're all inferior. I doubt he'll ever take a wife, but he does use one of the locals from time to time.''

''Use?'' Rikki said.

''Yeah. You know. Use,'' General Thayer elaborated. ''The Hounds bring one of the locals here, and the King, as he likes to put it, vents his biological urges. The type depends on his mood.''

''He rapes them?''

''Call it whatever you want. He gives them gold in exchange for their services.''

''Tell me,'' Rikki said. ''Do the men rape the women in Sparta?''

General Thayer looked at the martial artist. ''Of course not. A Spartan woman would slit the throat of anyone who tried, and the Spartan men would track any offender to the ends of the earth.''

''Odd,'' Rikki commented.

''What's so odd about that?'' General Thayer quizzed.

''Nothing,'' Rikki responded. ''I was referring to you.''

''Me?''

''Yes. You wouldn't tolerate anyone trying to force his

way on a Spartan woman, but you stand by and do nothing while the King rapes Memphis women.''

General Thayer drew up short and glared at the Warrior. ''Damn you! There you go again, trying to turn me against the King! Don't try my patience.''

''I merely made an observation.''

''Bullshit. I won't warn you again,'' General Thayer vowed. ''Stay off my case.''

Rikki said nothing.

''Move it,'' Thayer said, grabbing the Warrior by the left shoulder and shoving.

As he stumbled forward, Rikki grinned. He'd struck a raw nerve in the Spartan, found an opening he might be able to capitalize on later. He stopped and straightened next to a door on the right-hand side.

General Thayer moved to the door and knocked loudly twice.

''Enter, General,'' called out someone in the room beyond.

General Thayer twisted the knob and stepped within the throne room.

''You, too,'' Sergeant Boynton said, prodding the martial artist with the HK-33.

Rikki-Tikki-Tavi walked through the doorway, his senses fully primed, believing he was prepared for anything.

He was wrong.

CHAPTER NINE

"Watch out!" Chastity cried. "There's a hole!"

Blade braked and stared at the shallow rut in the roadway. "I doubt we'll fall in," he remarked sarcastically.

"I don't want to lose my daddy if you hit another hole," Chastity chastised him.

Sighing, Blade accelerated slowly.

"The kid has a point," Bonnie commented. "That last hole you managed not to miss almost sent me through the roof."

I wish it had! Blade almost replied, but he held his tongue. He glanced to his right. Chastity was beside him, then Bonnie and Clyde. The bazooka, snug in its crate, was propped between Clyde and the passenger door. "How far until Memphis?"

"About a half-mile," Bonnie replied. "We want to take a left up ahead and stick to the back roads all the way into downtown Memphis."

"I hope you're as good as your word," Blade mentioned.

"Trust me," Bonnie said, smiling.

Blade leaned over the steering wheel and shouted. "Anything, Hickok?"

"Nothin' yet, pard," the gunman responded from his post at the .50.

"Keep your eyes peeled," Blade advised.

"Aw, shucks. I thought I'd catch forty winks," Hickok quipped.

Chastity giggled. "Isn't my daddy funny?"

"A regular comedian," Blade said.

"Why can't you be funny like him?" Chastity inquired.

Blade was about to answer when he saw the cluster of long, low structures several hundred yards distant on the right side of the highway. Former warehouses? Or another shopping mall? He never could understand the prewar mania for shopping. If all of the malls and stores he'd seen on his travels were any indicator, then Americans must have spent practically all their free time buying things. Why? Was it because Americans had grown accustomed to having their needs supplied by others? Their entertainment, their clothing, even their food had been provided by specialized industries. Had the American people grown lazy?

He recalled a speech given by one of the Family Elders on the state of the United States prior to World War Three. The Elder presented an eloquent case criticizing America's citizens for failing to cultivate the rugged independence of their forefathers. Americans, the Elder opined, had lost track of their spiritual roots and substituted the collecting of material objects as a measure of self-worth instead of the possession of noble personal traits.

Blade's reflection was abruptly dissolved by a yell from above.

"Something on the right!"

His grey eyes narrowing, Blade applied pressure on the brake and scrutinized the road in front of them. A second later he spotted the fender, or part of one, jutting past the corner of the second of the four low structures.

"It could be part of an old wreck," Bonnie guessed.

"I don't recall seeing a wreck there before," Clyde commented.

Blade stopped and put the half-track in neutral. "I'm going to investigate. Stay put."

"I'll come with you," Bonnie offered.

"Read my lips," Blade said. "Don't get out of the cab." He took the M-10 from the dashboard, opened his door, and dropped to the ground.

"Want some company?" Hickok asked.

"Cover me," Blade directed, and advanced vigilantly, cradling the M-10 on his right hip. He'd feel foolish if the fender did belong to a wreck, but he'd be dead if they were driving into an ambush and he didn't take the time to check. Better safe than sorry, as the adage went. There were more lives at stake than his.

"Be careful, Uncle Blade," Chastity called.

So much for secrecy. He took another stride, then halted, listening. A weather-battered frame house was situated in the center of a weed-choked yard to his right. Trees filled the backyard and lined the edge of the highway. Wildlife should be in evidence. Birds. A squirrel or two. At the very least, insects.

There were none.

Blade approached the fender, estimating he had 60 or 70 yards to go. He scanned the roofs of the structures, the broken windows and the gloomy doorways.

If the Hounds were there, they were well hidden.

Fingering the trigger of the M-10, Blade covered five yards. With his attention focused on the fender and the low structures, he missed the motion in a tree to his right.

But Hickok didn't.

"It's a trap!" the gunman bellowed, and the .50 boomed.

Blade dove for the asphalt, scuffing his elbows and knees in the process. He looked to the right in time to behold the machine gun's heavy slugs rip through the foliage of an oak tree. Leaves and limbs were torn to pieces, and surpassing the blasting of the .50 was the rising scream of a falling Hound.

The sniper slammed into the ground with a crunch, his M-16 clattering onto the road.

An engine roared to life, and the fender protruding past

the second structure swept into view attached to a jeep filled with four Hounds. Three of them were armed with automatic rifles, and they cut loose at the half-track.

Blade pressed the M-10 to his right shoulder and fired, elevating the barrel to compensate for the range. He saw his rounds tear into the jeep's grill, and the vehicle swerved as the driver briefly lost control.

The three Hounds shifted their weapons, aiming at the giant.

Blade rolled to the right, then rose to his knees, ejecting the spent magazine and inserting another. The main disadvantage to an M-10 was its high cyclic rate. At up to 1150 rounds per second, the M-10 could empty a 30-round magazine in one and a half seconds. Insuring every shot counted was imperative.

Again the jeep swerved, toward the Warrior.

His lips a compressed line, Blade raised the barrel and sent half a magazine into the jeep's windshield.

Glass cracked and splintered, and the driver threw his arms in the air and slumped down. Unguided, the jeep veered sharply to the left. One of the Hounds in the rear tried to grip the wheel, his body sprawled over the top of the front seat and the dead driver, but his frantic lunge was for naught. The jeep careened into a tree with a tremendous crash, then flipped onto its side, spilling the Hounds. One man in black was flipped, headfirst, into a nearby trunk, his skull splitting with the ease of a rotten puffball. The other two landed intact, rising to a crouch and aiming at the giant.

Blade flattened both with a quick burst.

For a second there was lull, the only sound the hissing from the jeep's ruptured radiator. And then all hell broke loose.

Three jeeps and a truck, a troop transport, hurtled from concealment behind the four low structures. The truck rumbled across the highway and halted, becoming a make-shift roadblock. Hounds jumped from the bed and fanned out, forming a skirmish line, as the three jeeps sped toward the half-track.

Blade knew he'd be cut to ribbons out in the open. He dashed to the right side of the road, firing the last of the rounds in his magazine, and darted for cover in the shelter of an oak. With a deft flip of his left hand he discarded the empty clip and slapped in another. He glanced at the half-track, his eyes widening as the motorized behemoth was shifted into gear and driven forward.

Bonnie was driving!

He took a stride, seeing the bewildered expression on Hickok's face. There was no sign of Clyde and Chastity. Bonnie's countenance was a mask of grim determination as she hunched over the steering wheel. He was about to try and intercept the half-track, but the ground at his feet suddenly sprayed over his boots and he was compelled to flatten against the oak.

The three jeeps were now abreast and closing on the half-track at top speed, the Hounds shooting indiscriminately.

Blade could hear the metallic smacking of the rounds peppering the cab. He expected Bonnie to swerve to minimize the target she presented to the Hounds. Swerving would be the smart thing to do to save her skin. Instead, Bonnie held the half-track on a straight course, and Blade realized she was holding the armored vehicle steady so Hickok could fire accurately.

And fire he did.

The .50-caliber machine gun raked the highway from left to right, its heavy slugs tearing into the three jeeps, causing one to explode in flames when the fuel tank was struck. Out of control, with all four Hounds in the vehicle ablaze, the stricken jeep angled into the path of the jeep occupying the middle of the highway. The collision spun the second jeep around, and three Hounds slammed onto the cracked asphalt. Out of commission, smoke billowing from its ruined engine, the second jeep drifted to a stop five yards from the first, which was now a crippled inferno.

Leaving the third and last jeep. The driver weaved back

and forth, his three companions blasting away, and slanted to the edge of the highway, intending to pass the half-track on the driver's side. His purpose was clear; he wanted to give his companions an unobstructed shot at Bonnie.

Blade sighted the M-10, but before he could squeeze the trigger an unexpected development turned the tide.

Clyde appeared at the half-track windshield, the bazooka on his right shoulder and pointed at the approaching jeep.

In order to avoid obliteration, the driver reacted instinctively, jerking the steering wheel and sending the jeep into a screeching skid. Thrown off balance, the three with automatic rifles clutched at anything for support. They were unable to train their weapons on the half-track as the jeep swept past. The driver skillfully whipped the jeep in a tight U—turn for a second run.

Hickok had other ideas. He popped up at the tailgate, a Python in each hand, and the Colts boomed four times in rapid succession. With each shot a Hound toppled from the jeep—except for the driver, who stiffened, arched his back, and died.

Blade heard the grinding of gears and looked at the troop transport. Some of the Hounds were clambering onto the bed as the driver endeavored to move the truck from the half-track's path. Other, braver Hounds were firing at the on-rushing colossus.

Hickok mowed the exposed Hounds down with a sweep of the .50, then pivoted and leveled the machine gun at the truck, punching holes in the cab and the canvas covering the bed. The transport driver thrashed and sank from view, and agonized shrieks of the dying arose from the bed. The gunman sent round after round into the truck, reducing the canvas to shreds, as the half-track braked. Only when the ammunition was exhausted did the gunfighter stop.

The half-track, its engine sputtering and coughing, was less than ten yards from the transport.

Hefting the M-10, Blade sprinted forward.

Hickok was surveying the carnage, insuring the Hounds

were finished. He looked at Blade as his friend drew near.
"Where the blazes were you? Takin' a leak?" So saying,
he jumped to the ground.

Blade ignored the quip and stepped to the cab. "Is everyone
all right?" he asked, pulling the passenger door open.

Clyde was leaning on the dash with his left hand and braced
the bazooka with his right. His face was ashen, and he licked
his lips as he gazed at the Warrior. "It wasn't loaded," he
said weakly. "I was bluffing."

"You did fine," Blade said, complimenting him.

Beside Clyde, just scrambling up from the floor, was
Chastity. "Where's my daddy?" she inquired fearfully.

"Right here, princess," said the gunman, moving closer
to the seat.

Chastity climbed over Clyde's lap and leaped into the
gunman's arms.

Blade stared at Bonnie. She was sagging on the steering
wheel, sweat beading her forehead. "How about you?"

"I'm hunky-dory," Bonnie replied in a caustic tone.

"Where'd you learn to drive?" Blade queried.

Bonnie looked at him. "We found an antique clunker once
in drivable shape. It lasted about four months, as I recall.
We siphoned gas from an underground tank at a run-down
station. The gas smelled terrible and the car ran like sh—"
She checked herself. "Crud. But we had fun tooling around.
Genius, here, got the car running." She nodded at her
brother.

The half-track was belching dark smoke from its exhaust,
and the motor was clanking and clunking.

"This contraption is on its last legs," Hickok remarked.

In confirmation of the gunman's observation, there was
a loud bang and the engine was still.

"What did I tell you?" Hickok said.

Bonnie turned the key, but nothing happened. She tried
several times with the same result. "Dead," she declared.

"Want me to take a look at it?" Clyde offered.

Blade noted the dozens of bullet holes pockmarking the

hood and the grill, then crouched to peer at the puddles forming underneath the vehicle. "The half-track isn't going anywhere," he announced, and straightened, scanning the highway. The troop transport was a hopeless case, its motor destroyed by the .50. Two of the jeeps were on fire, and the third was on its side, its front end crushed. With the dead driver's lifeless eyes fixed on the sky, the fourth jeep was crawling toward the left side of the road, its engine idling. "I'll be right back," he said, and ran to catch the jeep.

The loss of the half-track was both good and bad. Without the armored vehicle's firepower, he knew they would be hard pressed to oppose the Hounds. On the other hand, the jeep would enable them to reach downtown Memphis faster, and if they were spotted the jeep gave them greater getaway speed. Another idea occured to him. If they survived the upcoming conflict with the Hounds, and if they could manage to keep the jeep intact, in another week they could be back at the Home with their loved ones.

The prospect brought a smile to his lips.

Absence, so the adage went, made the heart grow fonder. In this instance he agreed. He missed his wife and son unbearably, and he was aware that Hickok and Rikki missed their loved ones equally as much. When people were separated from those dearest to their hearts, he mentally noted, the separation accentuated their love like nothing else could.

What in the world was he doing?

Blade shook his head, irritated with himself. Now was hardly the time to dwell on his family. First things first. First he had to rescue Rikki from the Hounds, then journey over a thousand miles through the hostile Outlands, warding off mutants and scavengers every mile of the way.

Oh.

Was that all?

CHAPTER TEN

"Damn!" General Thayer muttered. "Not again."

"So what have we here, General?" demanded the sole occupant of the chamber in a high-pitched voice.

Rikki-Tikki-Tavi, standing on Thayer's right, scrutinized the spacious room, taking his bearings. A huge chandelier supplied ample lighting. All four walls were covered with large, colorful posters of men and women, some singly, others as part of a group, and the majority were playing musical instruments. The musicians displayed a preference for black leather clothing. A soft, thick green carpet covered the floor. In the middle of the chamber a dais had been erected, a circular platform consisting of four polished mahogany steps and a magnificent gilded throne.

"Don't be bashful, my dear Thayer," said the man seated on the throne. "Come. Come." He gestured, beckoning them to approach.

"I don't believe it," Sergeant Boynton exclaimed softly.

Rikki was likewise surprised, and he studied the man as he advanced.

The King was a model of contrasts. On the one hand, he was a strapping, muscular man well over six and a half feet tall, with short black hair, a trimmed mustache, and a Vandyke beard. On the other, he was wearing totally incongruous attire: red, spiked, high-healed shoes; black, fishnet stockings; and a lacy, slinky red dress. Thanks to excessive makeup, his lips were a bright red, his cheeks pink.

General Thayer halted at the base of the dais and saluted. "We have a prisoner for you, sir."

"So I see," the King stated, resting his chin in his right hand and inspecting the Warrior. "Where did you find him?"

"We were on a routine patrol southeast of the city," General Thayer detailed. "He walked into an ambush we set."

The King smiled at Rikki. "You're a bit on the small side, but maybe you're big where it counts," he said, and winked.

Rikki, for one of the very few times in his entire life, was dumbfounded.

"Was he alone?" the King asked.

"No, sir. There were two men and a child, a girl, with him," General Thayer answered.

His forehead creasing, the King made a show of looking around the Throne Room. "How odd. I don't see any of them."

"They escaped," General Thayer said sheepishly.

The King suddenly straightened, his green eyes locked on the Spartan. "Oh? Such inefficiency is inexcusable."

"I know," General Thayer admitted.

"Did we sustain any casualties?"

General Thayer mumbled a response.

The King leaned forward. "I'm sorry. My hearing must be going. I didn't catch that."

Thayer squared his shoulders and looked up. "Yes, sir. We lost twenty-nine men."

Rikki saw the King's face flush scarlet, and for several seconds it appeared as if the King was about to explode. Instead, the rulers's eyes narrowed and he spoke icily.

"Twenty-nine?"

"Yes, sir," General Thayer said. "But don't worry. I've sent a platoon to deal with the other two men and the girl."

"Why should I worry, my darling general?" the King asked. "Just because three years of hard labor were required to muster one hundred and twenty volunteers into my army? Just because, in one day, in one fight with *three men and a child,* you have succeeded in allowing almost one-fourth of the Hounds to be wiped out? Is that sufficient cause to worry?''

General Thayer did not respond.

The King rose slowly, his fists clenched. "I'll worry if I damn well want to worry!" he snapped. "I will not allow my timetable to be disrupted by your carelessness!"

Thayer stared at the floor.

"Look at me!" the King bellowed.

The Spartan complied.

"When I appointed you as my commander in chief, I assumed I was appointing a man of competence. After all, you were a highly ranked official in Sparta." The King paused, glowering. "I even overlooked the report of your breach of Spartan discipline. And what do I get for my compassion? An incompetent who can't defeat three men and a little girl!"

"They're the ones from St. Louis," General Thayer declared.

"What?"

"The pair we heard about," General Thayer said quickly. "The two who beat the Leather Knights. This is one of them."

Cocking his head, the King scrutinized Rikki. "He is? Why didn't you say so before?" He descended the dais to the bottom step and stood in front of the Warrior. "You don't strike me as being very formidable."

"He is, sir. Take my word for it," General Thayer said.

"What's your name?" the King demanded.

"Rikki," the martial artist answered.

"And where are you from?"

Rikki kept silent.

"He won't tell us a thing, sir," Thayer stated.

Rikki gazed at the bushy black hairs bristling over the

King's chest and protruding from the top of the red dress, his features impassive.

The King unexpectedly smiled. "There's no need to be obstinate with me, little man. We can be friends." He reached out and traced his right forefinger along the Warrior's chin.

And Rikki suddenly understood an earlier comment by General Thayer: "The Hounds bring one of the locals here, and the King, as he likes to put it, vents his biological urges. The type depends on his mood." *The type depends on his mood.*

"If you've fought the Leather Knights, then your enemies are my enemies," the King was saying. "The Knights have been a thorn in my side for too long. I intend to bring them to their knees. We can work together."

"No," Rikki said.

The King blinked rapidly in disbelief. "No?"

"No."

"You're refusing my generous offer before I've fully explained my terms?" the King snapped.

"I will not assist you," Rikki stated.

"But the Knights are your enemies," the King reiterated.

"You're mistaken," Rikki informed him.

The King placed his hands on his hips. "You *have* fought them before, haven't you?"

"Yes," Rikki responded. "But one fight does not mean they're my enemies. Temporary adversaries, would be more like it. The perfecting swordmaster embraces everyone in friendship, unless he is greeted with hostility. The Leather Knights were once my foes, but they might receive me cordially were I to pay St. Louis a visit now."

Grinning broadly, the King gazed at Rikki in amazement. "The perfecting swordmaster—!" he said, and laughed heartily.

"I've never seen anyone use a sword like he does," General Thayer commented.

The King glanced at the general's right side. "Is that his

sword?''

"Yes, sir.''

With an imperial air, the King extended his left hand.

General Thayer drew the gleaming katana and gave the sword to the ruler.

"Superb. Simply superb,'' the King remarked, hefting the katana. "Such intricate craftsmanship. Where did you obtain this?''

'It was bequeathed to mc by those I'm pledged to protect,'' Rikki detailed.

"And who, pray tell, might they be?''

"I cannot say.''

"There are ways of forcing you to talk,'' the King said. He pointed at a door in the center of the right-hand wall. "The Dark Lord can extract the information.'' He paused and smirked. "Have you heard about the Dark Lord?''

"Yes,'' Rikki acknowledged.

The King studied the Warrior for over a minute, and his smirk vanished. "You are different than most men. I don't detect any fear in your eyes.''

"Fear is a delusion,'' Rikki said. "To one with faith, there can be no fear.''

"Faith?'' the King repeated, snickering. "Whose faith? Yours or mine? Faith in what? In a god or in the workings of nature?''

"Faith in the Spirit.''

The King pursed his red lips. "You intrigue me, little man. I find you to be a pleasant diversion from the drudgery of greatness. I want to know you better.''

"I request to be released,'' Rikki said. "I am traveling through this territory in peace. Your men attacked me without provocation.''

"You were caught in *my* territory,'' the King declared. "Accordingly, you are subject to my will. I'll decide your fate.''

"I must warn you,'' Rikki mentioned. "I will escape, and more of your men may be harmed. You can prevent further bloodshed by setting me free.'' He paused. "If you don't release me, you also risk the wrath of my friends. They'll come after me, and if they arrive in Memphis while I am still in your custody, they'll slay everyone who stands in their way.''

"Should I tremble now or later?" the King quipped.

General Thayer looked at the Warrior with a worried expression. "My platoon will stop your friends.''

"What will be, will be,'' Rikki said enigmatically.

The King returned the katana to the Spartan. "I want my guard doubled as an added precaution.'' He gazed at the small man, trying to read Rikki's stolid countenance. "Not that I believe you, you understand, little man?''

"Your reign will be a short one,'' Rikki predicted.

"Now who's mistaken?'' the King asked, ascending slowly to his throne. He seated himself with a flourish, clasping his hands in his lap. "My reign will last for decades, and I will be remembered as a great conqueror. Alexander the Great. Attila the Hun. And myself, Aloysius the First. Future historians will rank us as the three mightiest military men of all time.''

"Your name is Aloysius?'' Rikki queried.

"Aloysius is the name I have chosen, and none is more fitting. Do you know what it means?''

"No,'' Rikki admitted.

"I chose the name after my vision, and my name, like my presence, is sacred.''

"Vision?'' Rikki said.

Aloysius the First settled in his throne. "Over three years ago the vision came to me. At the time I was a lowly scavenger, a nameless vagabond like so many inconsequential others. I didn't even know the identities of my father and mother.'' He stared at the chandelier. "And then, late one night, after I took the acid, while I was tripping, the vision came to me and opened my mind.''

"What is acid?'' Rikki inquired.

"You've never used acid? LSD?''

"No," Rikki said.

"You must be from the moon," Aloysius commented sarcastically. "Everyone knows what acid is. It's a drug, a hallucinogenic. Have you ever used *any* drugs?"

"I've used herbs," Rikki said. "Our Healers administer them to remedy illness."

"Herbs?" The King snickered. "Acid isn't an herb, little man. Acid is a potent psychedelic, like mescaline. I've used both many times. But I never saw a vision like the one I had that night." He smiled, his voice lowering. "I saw my destiny revealed. I saw myself as the ruler of the world. I saw myself on a throne just like this one I had built, and every person on the planet was bowing at my feet, hailing me as their undisputed ruler." He looked at the Warrior. "What do you think of that?"

Rikki couldn't resist the opening. "Does the word insane mean anything to you?"

General Thayer tensed, taking an audible breath.

Sergeant Boynton glanced at the martial artist in dread.

To their surprise, Aloysius the First grinned. "I would expect such a reaction from someone with your limited mentality. How could you possibly comprehend my magnificence? I always knew, deep down, that I was special, that there was a higher destiny in store for me. And now, thanks to my vision, I am claiming my heritage."

Rikki looked at General Thayer. "And you serve this madman?"

Aloysius cackled. "Mad, am I? You pitiful moron. In three years I've accomplished the impossible. Look around you. Once this was an empty, abandoned mansion, but under my direction this estate has been restored to its former grandeur. I took the rabble of Memphis and transfɔrmed them into an unstoppable army—"

"I thought General Thayer trained your men," Rikki interjected.

"And who selected the good general as commander in chief?" the King demanded. "I did! I now control everything within fifty miles of my capital. In six months I'll control one hundred miles. In a year the Midwest will be mine."

"Never happen," Rikki said.

"Why not?"

"The Leather Knights and the Technics, to mention just two factions, will oppose you, and both outnumber your army. Then there's the Russians, the Freedom Federation—"

"The Knights and the Technics outnumber me now, but not for long. As for the Russians, they have their hands full governing the territory they took during the war. They won't interfere with me until it's too late." Aloysius leaned forward. "What do you know about the Freedom Federation?"

"The Federation is stronger than the Knights, the Technics, and your Hounds combined. They'll stop you if no one else does."

"You think so? Let's see how smart you are." The King paused. "I'm not as ignorant as you seem to believe. I know there are different groups in control of certain cities or areas, and I've heard stories concerning the Federation. Yes, I face stiff opposition. But it will all crumble before an army over a million strong."

"A million?"

"Yes," Aloysius the First declared, his eyes radiating a maniacal sparkle. "The first three years have proceeded slowly, because I've had to consolidate my forces and selectively pick my targets. We've wiped out dozens of small communities and towns, and we've defeated Technic and Leather Knight patrols. The word is spreading about us. More men have flocked to my banner in the past three months than in the previous years. And why? Because I'm taking my recruits from the largest group of people in the Outlands, the scavengers."

Rikki's brow creased as he contemplated the implications.

"I'm no fool, swordmaster. Sure, there are a few areas already under the control of one group or another, but there is more land not under any control whatsoever. The Outlands embrace more territory than the controlled lands. And who lives in the Outlands? The outcasts, the nomads, the looters and raiders, the scavengers. There are millions of them. Millions!''

The madman spoke the truth. Rikki gazed at the King with dawning insight. A Family Elder had once calculated there were three to four million people living in the Outlands, some living in farming or mining communities, but the vast majority homeless wanderers who roamed the land preying on anyone and anything.

''I can see you're beginning to appreciate my vision,'' Aloysius said, noting the Warrior's change in expression. ''If I can gather the scavengers to my banner, there will be no stopping me. The Hounds of Hades will sweep over the land like a horde of locusts, devouring everyone stupid enough to resist me. The word is spreading, even as we speak. I've sent messengers out to the farthest corners of the Outlands, bidding every able-bodied scavenger to enlist in my army, promising them a share in the spoils. They'll be flocking in from all over.'' He smirked. ''Do you still think I'm an idiot, swordmaster?''

''There is a method to your madness,'' Rikki conceded.

''Genius has often been labeled insanity by the simple masses.''

''Backing up a bit,'' Rikki said, ''there's something puzzling me.''

''What?''

''You say that your name, like your presence, is sacred?''

''Nobility is deserving of veneration,'' Aloysius the First declared, ''especially when the nobility borders on divinity.''

''You consider yourself divine?''

The King straightened. ''Once my destiny is manifest, everyone will recognize the truth.''

''But if you're divine, what does that make the Dark Lord?'' Rikki asked.

"I'm the Dark Lord's chosen disciple. I'm the anointed one," Aloysius said.

"Do you take your orders from the Dark Lord?"

The King scowled. "I take orders from no one. You might conceive of the Dark Lord as my advisor and executioner, responsible for terminating those who would besmirch my dignity."

"But the Dark Lord is not omnipotent," Rikki observed. "He only kills one victim at a time."

"One is enough," Aloysius the First stated, and stared at the door in the right-hand wall. "I'll tell you what. Since you're so curious about the Dark Lord, it's fitting that you meet him." He stood and motioned at General Thayer. "Bring the swordmaster. I want to see if his courage is a facade."

The madman laughed at some private joke.

And Rikki suddenly recalled another statement General Thayer had made: "The important thing to remember is that if the King takes you in to meet the Dark Lord, you'll never come out again."

CHAPTER ELEVEN

"It's a mistake, damn it!" Bonnie snapped.

"My decision is final," Blade informed her.

"We need it," Bonnie insisted.

"Do you have something against walking?" Blade asked.

"No," Bonnie replied, "but I don't like the idea of being ripped to pieces by dogs."

Blade hefted the AR-15 he had confiscated from a dead Hound. "There are dog packs in Memphis?"

"There are dog packs everywhere," Bonnie revealed. "They usually shy away from humans, probably because they've seen us kill other dogs. Dog stew is real popular."

"We leave the jeep here," Blade said, glancing over his right shoulder. They had driven three and a half miles from the ambush site and taken an unmarked exit. The jeep was parked in a deserted garage next to a dilapidated frame house, and Hickok was lowering the wooden door.

"All tucked in, pard," the gunman declared.

Chastity, standing to the gunfighter's right, took his hand in hers. "Stay close to me, Daddy. I don't like this place. It smells."

"Where I go, you go, princess," Hickok promised. He placed his left hand on the strap of the M-16 slung over his left shoulder.

"You don't know what you're doing," Bonnie stated.

"You'll get us all killed."

Blade pivoted to his left and gazed at her angry features. "We're not taking the jeep any farther." He didn't want to chance damaging the vehicle, not when the jeep was their means of returning to the Home.

"At least let's stick to the main highways," Bonnie suggested. "The dogs don't go near them."

"No."

Bonnie glanced at her brother, who was leaning against the corner of the garage with the bazooka cradled in his arms. "Talk to this turkey. Tell him!"

"He's the boss," Clyde said with a shrug.

"Big help you are," Bonnie remarked.

Blade faced to the northwest. "Lead the way," he directed her.

Bonnie turned and tramped off, her annoyance conveyed in her posture. An AR-15 was over her right shoulder, a pistol around her waist.

Clyde followed. His pockets were bulging with the rockets for the bazooka, and his pants swayed awkwardly as he walked.

"Have you figured out why she wants to tag along with us?" Hickok asked, stepping to Blade's left.

"Not yet."

The Warriors trailed the sister and brother, winding along the trash-filled streets and alleys. Many of the buildings they passed were decayed and crumbling. Rusted, derelict vehicles were everywhere.

Clyde slowed and waited for the Warriors to catch up. "Please forgive Bonnie," he said to them. "She's not herself."

"She's not very fond of the Hounds," Blade mentioned.

"She hates their guts," Clyde said.

"And all because one of them wanted to go to bed with her, and he rigged the Hound physical against you?" Blade commented skeptically.

"There's more to it than that," Clyde responded.

"Did the Hound she mentioned, Sergeant Boynton, molest her?" Blade probed.

"No, he didn't."

"Then what's her real mission?" Blade queried.

"I can't say."

"We'll keep our lips sealed," Hickok chimed in.

"You'll have to ask Bonnie. I promised her I'd never tell a soul," Clyde divulged, and quickened his pace to reach his sister.

"Hmmmmmm," Hickok said.

"I agree," Blade observed.

As they progressed deeper into Memphis, the mounds of refuse became more numerous, the condition of the buildings deteriorated drastically, and the sickening stench intensified.

"How do folks live in this pigpen?" Hickok asked as they crossed a street and entered a gloomy alley.

"Is your Home like this?" Chastity inquired.

"Are you kiddin'?" Hickok rejoined. "This dump makes our Home look like Heaven. Our buildings are kept in tiptop shape, and we burn all of our garbage and trash." He paused. "You'll like the Home, princess. There are dozens of young'uns to play with, the Weavers will make you fine, new clothes from the fabric we've received in trade with the Civilized Zone, and you'll get three squares a day."

Chastity glanced up at the gunman. "Why would I want three squares?"

"I meant food," Hickok explained.

"You eat square food?"

"Not square food," Hickok said. "Three square meals a day. It's an old saying."

"Oh," Chastity responded, and was quiet for 30 seconds. "Why are your meals square? What kind of food do you eat?"

Hickok sighed and looked at Blade. "Why don't you lend me a hand?"

"Wouldn't think of it," Blade said with a smile. "You're doing just fine by yourself."

"Thanks, pard."

"So what's a square meal?" Chastity persisted.

"I told you. A square meal is an old expression," Hickok elaborated. "When you eat a square meal, you eat your fill. You'll never go hungry at the Home. Do you understand now?"

"I think so."

"There are dozens of sayings that have been around for ages," Hickok went on.

"Like what?" Chastity queried.

"Oh, like you can't teach an old dog new tricks," Hickok said.

"Why not?"

Blade chuckled.

"I suppose you could teach an old dog a new trick," Hickok stated.

"But you just said you can't," Chastity responded.

"I know. But I was usin' an example of a saying," Hickok said. "You can't teach an old dog new tricks."

"But you just said you could. I'm confused," Chastity remarked.

"That makes two of us," Hickok declared, exasperated.

"Can you teach an old dog new tricks?" Chastity asked.

"I don't know. I don't care. I'm sorry I ever brought the blasted thing up," Hickok mumbled.

"Maybe we could try," Chastity suggested.

"Try what?"

"Try to teach an old dog a new trick."

Blade beamed at the gunman, who promptly glared back.

"What about him?" Chastity queried.

"Who?" Hickok replied, gazing at her.

"That dog," Chastity said, and raised her left hand to point.

The Warriors looked up and froze.

Balefully eyeing them from the second floor of a four-story structure on their left, its canine features framed in a window long since shattered, was a gray and black mongrel.

"Maybe it's alone," Hickok commented.

Blade glanced to their rear. "No such luck."

Three dogs were 30 feet to the rear, standing close together, their mouths slightly open, their tongues and fangs visible.

Hickok looked back, then scooped Chastity into his left arm. "Four isn't so bad. We can take four, no sweat." He stared ahead to find Bonnie and Clyde stopped in their tracks by the sight of five dogs blocking the mouth of the alley 20 feet beyond.

Bonnie sighted her AR-15.

"No!" Blade called.

She turned, perplexed.

"The shots will alert the Hounds," Blade said, advancing slowly, warily watching the dog in the window as he passed underneath.

"I warned you this would happen," Bonnie reminded him. "How do you expect us to get out of this mess without firing a shot?"

"I'll take care of the dogs," Blade informed her.

"All by yourself?"

"You can help if you want, but no firing," Blade directed. He scanned the alley, spying a recessed entry or exit eight feet to the left. "Get in there. Move!"

The brother and sister hastily obeyed, stepping into the narrow space between the alley and a closed, pale green door. On their heels, alertly regarding the canines, came the Warriors.

Bonnie tried the doorknob. "It's locked."

"Break it in," Blade ordered.

The dogs on both sides began to pad forward.

"Here they come," Hickok announced, drawing his right Colt.

"Remember," Blade reiterated. "No shooting if we can help it."

"How do you plan to stop them?" Bonnie cracked. "With

your breath?''

Blade glanced at her, his eyes narrowing. ''Break down the door. Now.'' He slung the AR-15 over his left shoulder and drew both Bowies, then positioned himself in the opening to the alley.

''And be quick about it,'' Hickok added, feeling uncomfortable wedged in the middle with little room to maneuver.

Bonnie applied her right shoulder to the door.

''Lend her a hand,'' Hickok said, nudging Clyde with the Python.

''Are the dogs coming, Uncle Blade?'' Chastity asked.

''Yep,'' Blade confirmed, looking to the right and left. The mongrel in the window had disappeared, but the other eight were converging on the entryway, padding softly, their heads held low, their lips curled back. He crouched, gripping the Bowie hilts tightly, grateful the dogs would not be able to rush him en masse. The cramped confines would hinder their attack. He heard the thumping of Bonnie's and Clyde's shoulders against the door.

And the canine pack charged.

Galvanized into motion by a bestial growl from a Doberman pinscher on the left, all eight hurtled toward the giant.

Blade took them as they came, arcing his right Bowie into the first to reach him, a stubby mixed breed with oversized teeth that leaped at his midriff. He met the dog with the point of his Bowie, burying the knife in the breed's neck, the impact jarring his right arm. Blood gushed over him as the dog thrashed and gurgled, and he savagely tossed the dying animal from him with a sweep of his steely right arm.

The second dog never missed a beat. A grungy Samoyed, its white hair matted and filthy, snapped at the Warrior's ankles.

With a swiftness belying his size, Blade shifted his boots a few inches backward, evading the Samoyed's raking teeth, even as he swung his left arm down and in, the Bowie catching the dog in the left eye, slicing into the orb and shearing off flesh, hair, and the Samoyede's left ear in the bargain.

Howling in anguish, the Samoyede staggered off, crimson spurting the alley.

Blade straightened in time to take the largest dog head-on. A brindle-colored Bull Mastiff, over 30 inches high at the shoulders, 110 pounds of feral fury, snarled and went for his throat. He managed to get his left forearm in front of his neck, sweeping his arm under the mastiff's slavering jaws, momentarily holding the animal at bay, long enough to sink his right Bowie into the dog's chest.

Once.

Twice.

Three times.

The Bull Mastiff yelped and toppled to the left, sprawling at the Warrior's feet, briefly deterring the remaining pack members.

Blade glanced over his left shoulder at Clyde and Bonnie, who were still endeavoring to batter the door in. "Hurry!" he urged, then faced the growling dogs.

"We're trying," Bonnie said.

"Not hard enough," Hickok snapped, smacking her on the left arm with his Colt. "Move aside!"

Scowling, Bonnie leaned away from the door. Clyde did the same.

Hickok drew his right knee up to his waist and lashed out, planting the heel of his right moccasin next to the rusted doorknob. There was a loud snap, but the door held. Holding Chastity securely in his left arm, the gunman kicked once more, and was rewarded by cracks appearing in the wood panel.

Behind the gunman, Blade tensed, waiting for the pack to renew its assault. Oddly, the dogs were snarling and barking, their hair bristling, and staying out of the range of his Bowies.

Why weren't they pressing their attack?

The answer was revealed seconds later.

Grunting with the exertion, Hickok delivered another kick to the door, grinning as the wood around the lock splintered and the door swung inward into a murky corridor.

Filled with dogs.

CHAPTER TWELVE

"You'd better hope the Dark Lord is in a generous mood today," Aloysius the First remarked as they approached the red door in the right-hand wall.

Rikki walked behind the madman, with General Thayer at his right elbow and Sergeant Boynton at his left.

"In a minute you will understand why none dare oppose me," the King boasted.

"Sir, may I speak?" General Thayer said.

"Of course, my dear general," Aloysius the First replied.

"Is this wise, sir? I mean, what if the Dark Lord kills this man? We need reliable information on St. Louis before we launch our strike. . . ." Thayer stated, and checked himself, too late.

The King halted abruptly and wheeled, looking from Thayer to Boynton and back again. "General, how could you?"

"Sir?"

"You know our planned strike on St. Louis is classified information," Aloysius declared angrily.

"Yes, sir," General Thayer said. "But Sergeant Boynton already knows about it."

"He does?" Aloysius responded in a surly tone.

"Yes, sir. I confided in him. Sergeant Boynton is a trustworthy Hound."

"Have you informed anyone else?"

General Thayer hesitated, thinking of the driver of his jeep who had undoubtedly overheard the conversation en route to the city. "No, sir," he lied.

The King smiled at Sergeant Boynton. "Then no harm has been done, not if the sergeant is as trustworthy as you claim."

"I am, sir," Boynton blurted out.

"I'm sure you are," Aloysius said politely.

"If our prisoner is killed, sir," General Thayer resumed, "we'll lose the best chance we've got of discovering the Leather Knights' layout."

"Perish forbid," Aloysius responded, looking at the Warrior. "Very well. One last opportunity. Will you agree to provide the information I require?"

"Let me put it this way," Rikki answered, gazing idly at the posters decorating the wall, "don't hold your breath."

"Ever the defiant one, eh?" the King said.

Rikki stared at a blonde woman in a blue denim jacket and skirt, wearing dark glasses, seemingly endowed with . . . attributes the size of Mt. Everest.

"Do you like my collection?" Aloysius inquired.

"What are they?"

"Posters of prewar music stars," the King disclosed. "My Hounds are under standing orders to scour every music store they come across for posters. A lot of them are frayed or ripped," he said sadly.

Rikki studied the lunatic. "You have an interest in music?"

"Why would my musical affinity surprise you? Genius does not restrict itself to the mundane."

"Do you play an instrument?" Rikki asked.

"Yes," Aloysius said proudly. "The bongos."

"The bongos?"

"I found an intact pair in the basement storage room of a music store when I was fourteen, and I've been playing them ever since," Aloysius the First mentioned. "Musical instruments are rare in the Outlands, you know."

Rikki surveyed the dozens of posters on the wall,

marveling at the mix of men and women with their flowing, unkempt hair, garish attire, and sexually suggestive postures. Were they truly prewar musicians? Probably. They evinced the characteristic self-indulgent vanity so typical of prewar society, and were totally unlike the plain yet supremely talented Family Musicians. As part of his schooling, Rikki had been taught a Music Appreciation course by one of the Elders. His interest had been minimal, because as an aspiring Warrior he'd been more interested in martial matters. He could recall one part of the course he'd liked, a review of the music produced by a famous, outstanding American group known as Manheim Steamroller. Their music, as played by the Family musicians, had stirred his soul.

"I wanted to learn the guitar," Aloysius was saying, "but I could never locate anyone able to teach me. If I had, who knows? I might be a traveling minstrel today." He laughed at the idea. "No, I guess not. My destiny decrees otherwise."

"I have friends who are musicians," Rikki remarked. "They would be willing to teach you."

"They would?"

"If you will renounce your plans for conquest and disband the Hounds."

Aloysius the First cackled. "I *like* you, little man! You have a superb sense of humor. And what an intriguing choice. Fulfill my childhood dream of being a musician, and forsake my higher calling to tear down the vestiges of society and rebuild civilization in my image. How delightful." He suddenly sobered. "Enough of this frivolity."

"I take it your answer is no?" Rikki quipped.

"Let me make my position perfectly clear," Aloysius stated harshly. "I need information on the Leather Knights and St. Louis. You've been there and fought them, so you will willingly tell me what I want to know or I will have the Dark Lord grind the truth out of you."

Rikki stared at the King for a moment, an inexplicable sensation tugging at his mind, a feeling that the lunatic was deceiving him somehow. But how?

"Suit yourself," Aloysius snapped, and turned. He walked toward the red door.

Gazing at the posters as he was prodded by Sergeant Boynton, Rikki noticed a poster of the man portrayed in the painting on the landing. "Do you know his name?" he asked.

Aloysius glanced over his right shoulder. "Whose?"

"The man I saw in the painting," Rikki said.

They were within ten feet of the door when the King again stopped. "No, I don't. I wish I did. I found a document in an office upstairs bearing on the previous owners. The first was the man in the painting, who apparently was a real king. After his death the mansion was converted into a shrine, then later was bought by a musical group called The Blands. They converted it to their own use. Oddly enough, they kept his paintings but removed every reference to his identity. Perhaps they didn't like him, or the paintings were valuable. I don't know."

"He projects an aura of dignity," Rikki remarked, still looking at the man in the poster.

Aloysius the First nodded. "Yes. We have a lot in common." He proceeded to the door and placed his right hand on the knob.

Rikki held his hands at his waist as he walked over, mentally debating whether to make his break or wait. General Thayer was not being particularly cautious; the officer had his right hand on the hilt of the katana, but was otherwise unprepared for an unexpected bid for freedom. Sergeant Boynton, however, was covering Rikki with the HK-33. He decided to wait.

The King opened the red door a crack, then glanced at the noncom. "Sergeant, you will escort our prisoner inside."

Boynton gulped. "Sir?"

"You heard me. I want you to bring him in."

"But, sir—" Boynton began.

"Do as I say!" Aloysius barked, then looked at Thayer. "Is this the type of discipline you instill in my men?"

General Thayer stiffened. "The Hounds are trained to obey

you implicity.''

"If you can't train them acceptably, I'll find someone who can," Aloysius warned.

"I can train them, sir," General Thayer promised.

"We shall see." The King opened the door and stepped into a pitch-black chamber. "Bring the swordmaster in," he commanded, invisible in the stygian darkness.

Sergeant Boynton ushered the Warrior into the Dark Lord's sanctum.

"Close the door," ordered Aloysius's disembodied voice.

Boynton complied.

An ominous silence descended.

Rikki strained his physical senses to their utmost. His nostrils detected a slight tangy scent in the air, a peculiar odor that tingled his nose. Visually the chamber was impenetrable. Except for a faint rim of light around the edges of the door to his rear, the chamber was cast into complete blackness. He listened for the tapping of the King's high heels, but all he could perceive was a stealthy scuffing sound.

"Sir, are you there?" Sergeant Boynton asked nervously.

The King did not reply.

"Oh, shit," Sergeant Boynton muttered, glancing at the door. "This stinks."

"Where is the Dark Lord?" Rikki inquired.

"*I am here!*" thundered a raspy, low voice. "*Behold!*"

A pair of fiery red eyes materialized abruptly 20 feet above the floor and ten yards from the Warrior and the Hound.

"*Do you see me now?*"

"Yes!" Sergeant Boynton exclaimed in undisguised dread. "We see you, Mighty One."

"*Down on your knees, humans!*" the Dark Lord bellowed, and the air near the eyes crackled and sparked with vivid flashes of miniature lightning. Huge radiant spheres containing arcing purple and blue rays appeared on both sides of the eyes, with each glowing sphere 30 feet from those blazing orbs.

Sergeant Boynton threw himself on his knees, the HK-33 on the floor next to his bowed forehead. "I hear and obey, Dark Lord!"

Rikki smelled an acrid odor, the aroma of something burning. He tried to determine if the red eyes were gazing at Boynton or him, but the orbs, lacking pupils and never contracting or widening, gave the impression of being fixed on nothing and everything. He could hear a loud humming.

"*Both of you—kneel!*" the Dark Lord directed.

Sergeant Boynton looked up. "Kneel, you asshole," he hissed. "On your knees."

"I kneel to no one," Rikki declared.

"*You will kneel to me*," the Dark Lord stated.

"Never."

"*Resistance is futile. I could slay you where you stand,*" the Dark Lord observed. There was a metallic quality to his voice, and the words were clipped and precise.

"I will not kneel," Rikki vowed.

"Kneel, damn you, before he kills both of us," Sergeant Boynton snapped.

"Never," Rikki reiterated.

"That's what you think," Sergeant Boynton responded angrily, and before his intent could be gauged, he swept his right leg into the back of the Warrior's knees.

Taken unawares, Rikki buckled and fell backwards. He felt the noncom grab him and attempt to wrestle him into a kneeling posture, and he lashed out with his left elbow and caught Boynton on the chin.

The sergeant, on his knees but off balance, grunted as he was struck and swayed to the left.

Rikki followed through with another elbow jab to Boynton's chest, gouging the tip of his elbow into the Hound's ribs. He cupped his hands and delivered a powerful blow to the noncom's right cheek, and Boynton went down.

"*Cease and desist!*"

Sergeant Boynton, about to scramble to his knees, froze.

Rikki was on his left side. He rose slowly to his full height and stood, waiting.

"Why do you fight?" the Dark Lord demanded.

"I wanted him to kneel for you, mighty one," Sergeant Boynton answered.

"You wanted?"

"Yes, Dark Lord. I wanted to help you."

The response was blistering. *"And who are you, puny human? Did I request your aid? Do I need you to compel someone to kneel?"*

"No, Dark Lord—"

"I am the Dark Lord. I am power personified. I am what I am, and there are none like me."

"I know, Dark Lord—"

"No one can escape my wrath. Like a specter in the night, I seek out my enemies and make an end of them. My word is law, and my will is my blade of retribution."

Sergeant Boynton was trembling.

"Except for Aloysius the First, none are my equal."

Rikki could discern the vague outline of a large, bulky object or objects ten feet below the orbs. What were they?

"Do you doubt me?"

"No, magnificent one!" Sergeant Boynton cried.

"And what about you, swordmaster?"

The word caused Rikki to do a double take, and he stared at the fiery eyes in open-mouthed wonder.

"What about you?" the Dark Lord repeated.

"What about me?"

"Do you believe in my power?"

"True power stems from the Spirit. Where does your power stem from?"

"Observe and learn."

A raucous cacophony of sound blasted from the Dark Lord, a strident mixture of wailing, screeching tones, some individual notes attaining a crescendo of piercing intensity while others were plummeting to the depths of the auditory scale. The result was a deranged orchestration of deafening volume.

Rikki inadvertenly flinched, and he saw Sergeant Boynton cringing on the floor. His ears were ringing terribly. The intensity of the noise was painful to endure, and he wished his hands were free so he could protect his eardrums. The torment grew and grew, making his head pound in anguish. Just when the bizarre concert attained its most torturous level, two surprises occurred simultaneously.

The noise unaccountably ceased.

And the Dark Lord's chamber went totally dark.

A ringing engulfed Rikki's ears, the only sound in his universe. He looked for Sergeant Boynton, but the noncom was indistinguishable in the dark chamber. The next moment a hand clutched at his left ankle, catching on the fabric of his baggy pants, tugging fiercely. He started to resist, and as quickly as the tugging began, it stopped, the hand slipping from his clothing. "Boynton?" he said, startled by the faint, muffled quality to his voice.

The Hound did not reply.

"Boynton?"

"Sergeant Boynton is no longer with us," declared a familiar tenor to his rear.

Rikki turned as the red door was opened, and the influx of bright light made him squint and blink.

Aloysius the First was framed in the doorway. "The Dark Lord elected to give you a demonstration of his power," he said, nodding to the left.

His abdomen tightening in expectation, Rikki glanced down at the floor near his feet.

Sergeant Boynton's face was a grisly death mask, his features contorted, his tongue protruding from his mouth, his eyes wide and gaping, his cheeks distended.

Aloysius the First smiled at the Warrior. "Don't worry, little man. Your hearing will return to normal shortly."

Rikki stared at the dead Hound. There wasn't a wound

in sight. "This was unnecessary," he commented.

"To the contrary, swordmaster," the King responded. "This was essential to your education, to your mature appreciation of your situation. You've been granted a temporary reprieve. You have one hour to change your mind, to agree to tell me everything you know about the Leather Knights and their setup in St. Louis. If you still refuse at the end of the allotted hour . . ." He paused, smirked, and pointed at the corpse. "Guess who is next?"

CHAPTER THIRTEEN

Once they were "man's best friend." Once. Before the terrible devastation of World War Three. Before hundreds of thousands were abandoned and forced to forage for their food as their ancestors had done. Before the limited amount of game put their ever-burgeoning numbers into direct competition with their former masters. Before the primal survival of the fittest became, once again and perhaps for all time, the unwritten law of the land. Once they were cute and cuddly and pampered with prepared food from cans or boxes, and even clothed in attire reflective of their masters' warped tastes in fashion. Once.

But not now.

Now dog packs numbered well over a million canines, roaming the polluted and untainted landscape alike, constantly seeking prey to appease their ever-present hunger. Other than the bestial mutants, dog packs were the primary danger to travelers everywhere.

Blade knew this danger well; he had battled dogs on several occasions, and the prospect of another such struggle was singularly unappealing. Up until the moment Hickok kicked in the door, Blade had hoped to avoid a full-fledged engagement. At that instant, with the baying of the savage band as it closed in from both sides, his hopes were dashed on the brutal rocks of reality.

Chastity screamed for her life.

Clyde and Bonnie took the brunt of the attack from the dogs in the hallway, Clyde trying to beat them with the bazooka and Bonnie swinging her AR-15 as a club.

The dogs in the alley surged forward in unison, closing on the giant, their teeth snapping and slashing, trying to overpower the human by sheer force of numbers.

Towering above the five raging canines, his bulging muscles rippling with every skillful move, Blade ripped into them with his Bowies. The razor edges of his big knives sliced eyeballs, hacked off ears, chopped tongues, and slit flesh and hair with gory ease. Two of the dogs were dead in as many seconds, and the remaining three severely injured before they could retreat beyond the range of the Warrior's lethal weapons.

While Blade held off the five in the alley, his companions were not faring as well. A Rottweiler clamped its viselike jaws on Clyde's right leg below the knee, wrenching and twisting its head ferociously. Clyde cried out and doubled over, exposing his head and neck to the other dogs in the corridor. Out of the pack hurtled a Pit Bull, its pointed teeth chomping on Clyde's throat. He shrieked as blood sprayed from his severed vessels.

"Clyde!" Bonnie wailed, letting down her own guard and reaching for her brother.

A Husky pounced on her left arm, and she released the AR-15.

The hallway was a mass of barking, howling, bloodthirsty canines.

"Daddy!" Chastity shouted, clinging to the gunman's neck. "Do something!"

Stuck in the middle, screened by the others, Chastity in his left arm, a Python in his right hand, Hickok had obeyed Blade's injunction to avoid gunfire. But the sight of Clyde being torn to shreds, of Bonnie cursing as the husky chewed on her, and the terrified cry of his adopted daughter all conspired to rouse the gunfighter to action. He lowered Chastity quickly to the ground, placing her between Blade and himself, and then drew his left Colt. He faced the dogs in the corridor, his countenance seemingly chiseled in stone.

Clyde's neck resembled shredded venison.

Bonnie was striving to wrest her arm from the Husky.

The gray and black mongrel from the window sprang at the gunman.

Hickok shot the mongrel between the eyes with his right Python, the revolver blasting and bucking in his hand.

Catapulted backwards by the impact of the slug, the mongrel flipped onto the hall floor.

The gunfighter advanced on the dog pack, each step slow and deliberate, firing twice with every stride. His next pair of shots downed the Rottweiler and the Pit Bull; the two after that killed the Husky and a charging Collie. He moved past Bonnie, who was on her knees, her left arm pressed to her stomach, and thumbed back the hammers.

Panicked by the abrupt deaths of five of their number and the thundering of the Magnums, the canines were endeavoring to flee.

Hickok wasn't about to let them off so easy. He continued to walk forward, firing each Python once more, and yet again. With each shot a dog fell, four of them thrashing and whining as they died in pools of their spurting blood.

The rest of the dogs were clawing over one another in their frenzy to escape. Barking and baying, they fled through a door at the far end of the corridor. In seconds they were gone.

Hickok watched the last dog hightail it. He reloaded quickly, holstered the Colts, unslung the M-16, and turned, prepared to lend aid to Blade, but his friend had already dispatched the dogs in the alley and was staring at Clyde, frowning.

Chastity was leaning against the wall, sniffling.

A crimson river flowed from Clyde's neck. He was on his right side, his eyes glassy, his spectacles lying in the spreading crimson spring. Beside him, her knees immersed in his blood, oblivious to her own wound, crying softly, was Bonnie.

The gunman walked to her and squatted. "Bonnie?"

"Leave me alone," she said, her words scarcely perceptible.

"We can't stay here. The shots will bring the Hounds."

"Go on."

Chastity ran to the gunfighter, skirting Bonnie and flinging her slim arms around his neck. "Daddy! You're okay!"

"Fit as a fiddle," Hickok assured her.

Blade came over. "Bonnie, Hickok's right. We must get out of here."

"Go."

"You're coming with us," Blade said, wiping the Bowies on his pants.

"I'm not leaving my brother," Bonnie stated huskily.

"There's nothing we can do for him," Blade noted, his tone reflecting his sympathy.

"I'm not leaving," Bonnie insisted.

Blade slid the Bowies into their sheaths, then crouched. "The Hounds will catch you and kill you."

"I don't care."

"Let me see that arm."

"It's fine."

"Let me see," Blade said, reaching out and taking her left arm in his right hand. The husky had made a mess of the flesh near her elbow but, fortunately, had not torn open a vein or artery. "This must hurt," he commented.

Bonnie looked at her brother, her eyes streaming tears. "He didn't want to do this. He only came because of me."

"He loved you very much," Blade said.

She merely nodded and moaned.

"He wouldn't want you to waste your life," Blade mentioned.

"It's too late to turn over a new leaf," Bonnie responded in abject misery.

"We can't leave you," Blade said.

"I want to bury him."

"There's no time," Blade replied.

"You go on. I'll bury him and catch up when I can,"
Bonnie proposed.

"There's no time," Blade stressed.

Bonnie finally took her eyes from her brother and gazed
at the giant. "Get the hell out of here!"

Blade sighed and frowned. "I'm truly sorry for what I'm
about to do."

"What?"

Leaning forward, Blade scooped her into his massive arms
before she could resist. He stood and nodded for Hickok to
proceed down the hallway.

"Put me down, damn you!" Bonnie protested, kicking her
legs.

Blade ignored her and strode after the gunman.

"Put me down!"

"You're coming with us," Blade declared brusquely.

"You bastard!"

"There are some who would agree with you," Blade
quipped.

"Please!"

"No."

Bonnie glanced over his broad right shoulder at her
brother's body, then sobbed. "Oh, Clyde." She buried her
face in Blade's neck and wept uncontrollably.

The Warrior let her vent her emotions. He followed Hickok
through the door at the end of the corridor, finding another
hall leading to the right. They took the hall to a large room
caked with dust and filled with broken furniture. A broken
picture window fronted a narrow, deserted street.

"The mutts are long gone," Hickok remarked.

"Good," Chastity said.

A front door hung by one hinge, its paint chipped, its wood
warped.

Hickok barreled out the door and stopped on the sidewalk.
"Which way, pard?"

Blade scanned the filthy street. "We need a place to hole

up,'' he said, nodding to the right.

Hickok moved off, carrying Chastity.

"Blade?" Bonnie whispered as the Warrior hastened on the heels of the gunman.

"You don't need to say anything," he told her.

Bonnie raised her head. Glistening moisture covered her cheeks and chin. Her eyes were red and puffy, and her nose was running. "Yes, I do."

Blade scrutinized the buildings they were passing.

"I killed my brother," Bonnie declared.

"You're being ridiculous."

"He came along because of me," Bonnie said, and closed her eyes. "I'm responsible."

"Clyde was a grown man. He was responsible for his own actions."

"But I—" Bonnie began.

"Clyde came because he loved you," Blade said, cutting her off, his voice unusually stern. "The choice was his to make, and the consequences are his alone." He paused. "We all have decisions to make, dozens every day. Sometimes we make the right decisions, and sometimes we don't. Every action brings a reaction, and we must learn to bear the responsibility for the reactions our actions cause, for the consequences of our decisions. We can't blame others for our failures, and we can't blame ourselves for theirs. A man isn't a man, a woman isn't a woman, until they learn to bear the responsibility for their own decisions. Until then, they're no more than overgrown children." He paused again. "Your brother was not a child."

Bonnie gazed at him quizzically for a moment. "There's more to you than meets the eye."

"Can you walk now? I want my hands free in case we're attacked again."

"Oh, sure," Bonnie said self-consciously. "Sorry. You can put me down."

Blade gently lowered her to the asphalt. "You can manage? Are you positive?"

"No problem."

The Warrior unslung the AR-15 and extended the rifle. "Here."

"What's this for?"

"You left yours in the alley," Blade reminded her. "Take this."

She obeyed. "Thanks."

Blade resumed looking for a hiding place. "As soon as we stop, we'll tend to your wound."

"There's very little blood," Bonnie commented while inspecting her left arm. "I doubt there'll be an infection."

"You never know. Better safe than sorry."

They came to an intersection and trailed Hickok to the left.

"What happens after you find your friend?" Bonnie inquired.

"We're heading for our Home in Minnesota," Blade said.

"Is that far?"

"Do you know where Minnesota is located?"

"No," Bonnie replied sheepishly.

"Well, it's far enough," Blade stated. "Even with a jeep, and what with all the mutants and whatnot we'll run into along the way, we won't reach our Home for at least a week."

"You sound anxious to get back."

"Lady, you don't know the half of it."

"Is there someone there waiting for you?"

Blade nodded and smiled. "My Family."

"You have a woman?"

"A wife and a son," Blade said. "Jenny and Gabe."

Bonnie deliberately glanced to the right so he wouldn't notice her frown.

"Hickok is married too," Blade added. "You probably won't believe this, but he's a first-class husband and father."

She looked at the giant, her expression blank. "I believe you. Hickok impresses me as being the kind of man a woman can rely on."

"Oh?"

"I knew he was reliable when he threatened to—how did he put it?—ventilate my noggin."

Blade stared at her, clearly puzzled.

"I knew he was serious. I recognized that he's a man of his word. The honest type."

"Feminine logic never ceases to amaze me."

"I feel the same way about men," Bonnie confessed.

Blade checked to the rear, ensuring no one was pursuing them. "Since we're being so honest, maybe you would like to tell the truth about something else?"

"Like what?"

"Like the real reason you hate the Hounds?"

"I told you. One of them has the hots for me, and they wouldn't let Clyde . . ."

Blade held up his right hand. "Save your breath. I want to hear the truth."

"I'm telling the truth."

"And don't insult my intelligence."

Bonnie gazed at the giant. "Why won't you believe me?"

"I wasn't born yesterday. I've seen the hatred in your eyes when you mention the Hounds, and I know there must be a deeper reason than you've let on."

Her shoulders slumped and she stared absently at the tall structures marking the downtown Memphis skyline. "Your wife is a lucky woman."

"Why do you say that?"

"Oh, no deep reason," Bonnie said, mustering a feeble smile. "You're right. There is another reason I hate the Hounds."

"Care to talk about it?"

Hickok and Chastity turned right at the next intersection.

"It's very personal," Bonnie said.

"I understand," Blade responded.

They covered another yard, and had about seven more to go to reach the intersection.

"What do you know about the leader of the Hounds, about the King?" Bonnie inquired.

"Next to nothing," Blade admitted.

"Did you know he likes to rape his sexual partners?"

"Do you have this on reliable authority?"

Bonnie snickered. "The best. The son of a bitch raped me."

Stunned by the revelation, Blade gaped at her, seeing the distress etching her attractive features, feeling his heart go out to her, and comprehending her motivation for wanting to inflict as much damage as she could on the Hounds. "I didn't know," he blurted out, and he was still gawking at her as they rounded the corner. He saw her eyes widen in alarm and glanced straight ahead.

There were Hickok and Chastity, standing not ten feet away.

And 20 feet beyond them, strung across the street, armed to the teeth, was a six-man Hound patrol.

CHAPTER FOURTEEN

General Thayer was in a foul mood when he descended the stairs to the mansion basement. He ignored the salutes of the two guards posted at the base of the stairs and tramped along a tiled corridor until he came to the holding cell containing the prisoner. With a snap of his right wrist, he flicked open the small metal panel covering the barred window in the top portion of the door. He expected to find the stranger pacing the cell, nervously awaiting execution. Instead, the man called Rikki was seated, cross-legged, in the center of the cell, his eyes closed, his chin on his chest, his cupped hands on his knees. "Rikki-Tikki-Tavi?"

Rikki's eyes slowly opened, his head lifting. "Spartan."

"I need to talk to you," General Thayer said.

"I'm glad you're here," Rikki stated. "I neglected to thank you for having the guards remove the handcuffs."

"It was the least I could do," Thayer responded. "Your last hour on earth should not be spent in cuffs."

"I'm grateful for your concern."

"Sergeant Boynton's body was just carted off for burial," Thayer disclosed. "As always, I couldn't find any hint of the cause of his death."

"And you won't," Rikki said.

"Do you have some idea?"

"Perhaps."

General Thayer pressed his face to the window. "What did you see in there?"

"Very little."

"Did you see the Dark Lord?"

"I saw—something."

"Did the Dark Lord speak to you?"

"Someone did."

General Thayer's forehead furrowed in perplexity. "Why are you treating me this way?"

"What way?"

"You're not answering my questions."

"I've answered them."

Thayer sighed and shook his head. "You're different from most, you know that?"

"Each of us is unique."

"How can you be so calm at a time like this? In forty minutes the King will have you killed?"

"Someone will die," Rikki said.

"Damn you!" Thayer snapped. "I wish I'd never caught you. You're nothing but trouble."

Rikki scrutinized the Spartan's features. "Do I disturb you?"

"Disburb me? There's the understatement of the year. Yes, you disturb me. You remind me of a time when I held a higher set of values than I do now. You remind me of when I was a real man, and not second in command to a . . ." Thayer caught himself, then pressed his forehead to the bars.

"Be careful," Rikki said with a grin. "You don't want me to turn you against the King."

General Thayer failed to appreciate the humor. "Life was so much simpler in Sparta. My duty was clear."

"You were a military man in Sparta?" Rikki prompted, hoping to learn more about the new city-state.

Thayer nodded. "A captain in the royal bodyguard. Three hundred soldiers, the very best in Sparta, are assigned as bodyguards to the kings."

"Kings?"

"The Spartan constitution requires two rulers."

"Then your appointment to the royal bodyguard was quite an honor," Rikki deduced. "You must have been an outstanding soldier."

Thayer frowned. "I was, once. My name was engraved on the plaque of distinction. Now it's been removed, and I am prohibited from returning to Sparta forever. I can't even use my given name."

"Thayer is not your real name?"

"No. When a Spartan is banished, he is stripped of his Spartan identity. I took the name Thayer from a book."

"Was your banishment justified?"

General Thayer glanced at the Warrior in sadness. "Yes," he said softly. "My crime was heinous. There was a plot to assassinate one of the kings, and I was on duty with thirty men when the traitors struck. There were over forty of them, all from the lower classes. They crept over one of the palace walls and attempted to kill the king while he slept. One of my men sounded the alarm, and we engaged them." He smirked. "They were no match for Spartan superiority. We slaughtered them. I was guarding the king's door with several others, one of whom was my eldest son." He inhaled loudly, his shoulders slumping.

Rikki waited patiently for the Spartan to continue. Half a minute elapsed.

"One of the traitors shot my son," Thayer said, his tone laced with sorrow. "That's when I showed my weakness."

"Weakness?"

"Yes. I turned away from the king's door and ran to my son, just as another officer arrived with reinforcements. He saw my breach of discipline and reported my violation of regulations."

"You were banished because you aided your son?" Rikki asked in surprise.

"I was banished because I deserted my post. My orders were to defend the king with my life, to allow no one to enter his chambers without permission. My post was at that door. And when I saw my son shot, I abandoned my post.''

''Did your son live?''

Thayer shook his head.

''Your punishment was excessive,'' Rikki stated.

''My punishment was fair, even lenient,'' Thayer said, disagreeing. ''The judges could have sentenced me to death. Instead, I was formally sent into exile. I'm not permitted to ever return to Sparta, and my Spartan identity has been stricken from the official records. My disgrace was my own fault. Spartans are trained from birth to adhere to their duty above all else. I violated our basic credo.''

Rikki digested this information in thoughtful silence. The new Sparta, he reasoned, was remarkably similar to the ancient Sparta. Both, evidently, operated under a rigid military caste system. ''Where is Sparta located?'' he inquired casually.

''I told you before. I'm not at liberty to say.''

Rikki pursed his lips. ''Very well. I suppose it doesn't matter in the long run.''

Thayer looked at the martial artist. ''What do you mean?''

''Does Aloysius the First know Sparta's location?''

''Of course not. Do you think I'm nuts?'' Thayer queried rhetorically.

''I think you are very lonely and extremely miserable.''

General Thayer straightened. ''I don't need your sympathy, Rikki. I brought my fate on myself. I suffered the disgrace of banishment, and I wandered the Outlands for over a year before I signed on with the King. I have no one to blame but myself.''

''And will you blame yourself for Sparta's destruction?''

''Destruction?''

''Eventually the King will destroy Sparta.''

''He doesn't even know Sparta's location. How can he destroy something he can't find?''

''Aloysius will find Sparta sooner or later.''

"You're just saying that," Thayer declared.

"Am I? The King is insane, but his master plan has merit. If he succeeds in rousing every scavenger in the Outlands to his cause, he'll raise the largest army on the continent. There will be no stopping him. He'd probably roll right over the Russians. A solitary city-state like Sparta wouldn't stand a chance."

"Sparta is well hidden, off the beaten path."

"Even so, Aloysius will find it. Inevitably, as his power continues to grow, as the territory under his control spreads, he'll discover Sparta's location. Once he does, Sparta will fall to the Hounds of Hades."

"Never!"

"You're deluding yourself if you think otherwise."

"But I'm the commander of his army. He wouldn't conquer my people if I request they be spared."

"Aloysius wants to be undisputed ruler of the planet," Rikki observed. "Do you really believe he would allow Sparta to be independent of his authority?"

General Thayer chewed on his lower lip, his visage troubled. "But he'll never get that far. Someone is bound to stop him."

"Don't let him hear you say that."

"I've never believed his plans for world conquest would succeed," Thayer remarked. "I've never considered him a threat to Sparta."

"Aloysius is a threat to the entire planet," Rikki reiterated. "His deranged ambition will inflict suffering on countless lives."

The Spartan was engrossed in his own musings. "I signed on with the King because I wanted to prove myself. I've always known the Hounds will be defeated, sooner or later."

"You knowingly joined a losing cause?" Rikki queried.

General Thayer glanced at him. "I'd buried my past until you arrived. Now you're stirring memories better left forgotten."

"Why did you come to see me?"

"I was contemplating releasing you," Thayer divulged. "I could always say you escaped."

"Will you release me?"

'Not now. I want you out of my life. People like you are dangerous. You inspire others to follow your example of perfection."

Rikki grinned. "I'm far from perfect."

The former Spartan eyed the Warrior for a moment. "There's nothing else to say." He wheeled and stalked off.

His supple muscles uncoiling, Rikki stood slowly and moved to the door. General Thayer had neglected to close the panel over the barred window, allowing Rikki to see the pair of guards at the end of the corridor. He saw the officer disappear up the stairs, and the two Hounds exchanged muted words as they apparently discussed the general's behavior.

Forty minutes, Thayer had said.

Not a lot of time.

Rikki surveyed the holding cell, which contained a toilet facility in the far left corner of the room but was otherwise devoid of furniture and windows to the outside, and came to the conclusion clever measures were called for. He gazed at the guards briefly, then crouched, cupped his hands around his mouth, and uttered a strangled scream. After waiting a bit, he repeated the noise.

There wasn't long to wait.

Boot steps pounded on the tile floor.

"—hell was that?"

"I don't know," replied the second Hound.

"It sounded like he was hanging himself," suggested the first.

"There's nothing in his cell he could use to hang himself."

"Maybe he had something concealed in his clothes, something we missed."

"Shit. The King will have our hides if this guy is dead."

Rikki flattened on his stomach at the inner base of the door.

There was the sound of breathing at the barred window.

"Damn. I don't see him!" declared one of the guards.

"He's got to be in there."

"Look for yourself."

A shuffling noise was followed by an exclamation. "Son of a bitch! Get this door open."

Rikki heard a rattling in the lock as a key was inserted, and he edged away from the door until he was just beyond the radius of the farthest point of the door's anticipated inward sweep. If he was correct, the guard would fling the door open and miss him by a hair.

The key was twisted and there was a loud click.

A rush of air touched the Warrior's face as the door was shoved wide, and the first guard rushed into the holding cell. The Hound's left boot caught on Rikki's shoulder, and with a startled "Hey!" the guard tripped and fell.

"What the—!" blurted out the second Hound, about to enter the room.

Rikki was already in motion, swinging his feet around and in and slamming his heels into the knees of the second Hound. A sharp crack, a screech of pain, and the second Hound was toppling forward, trying to level the AR-15. Rikki deflected the barrel of the automatic rifle with his right forearm, then rammed a leopard-paw strike into the Hound's throat as the man came down.

The first guard, on his hands and knees, was scrambling to face the prisoner.

Rikki arched his back and sprang erect, spinning as he rose, delivering a kick to the tip of the first Hound's chin. The man grunted and sagged, and another kick rendered him insensate. Rikki glanced at the second guard, who was flat on his back, gasping and convulsing, his hands pressed to his crushed windpipe.

The Warrior disliked seeing his foe suffer.

With a precisely angled sword-hand chop to the Hound's nose, Rikki ended the man's misery.

No one else had appeared in the hallway.

Moving swiftly, Rikki grabbed the AR-15 and raced down the corridor to the stairs. He checked, verifying the safety was off, and ascended, a step at a time, all the while gazing overhead to insure more Hounds weren't stationed above him. What should he do now? He asked himself. Escape the mansion while the opportunity presented itself? Or try to slay Aloysius the First and terminate the madman's demented scheme for global domination? Either way, his main priority was reclaiming his katana. General Thayer must still be on the estate. Rikki doubted the officer would leave prior to the execution. Once he found Thayer and recovered the katana, he could decide which course to pursue.

A closed brown door blocked his path.

Rikki halted at the door and listened. He was about to reach for the doorknob when he heard voices approaching from the opposite side. Without hesitation he threw himself behind the door as it opened.

"—wants to talk to the prisoner again," General Thayer was saying.

"I wouldn't want to be in his shoes, sir," remarked one of the two Hounds accompanying the officer, both of whom had AR-15's slung over their right shoulders.

The door closed as they started down the stairs.

"Hello, Spartan," said someone in a low tone to their rear.

They whirled together, General Thayer's eyes widening in astonishment.

"You!" the Spartan exclaimed.

The two Hounds appeared thoroughly confounded, and neither made a move for their weapon.

Rikki held his automatic rifle loosely in his left hand, the barrel slanted downward. "I've come for my katana."

General Thayer was on the third step. The pair of guards were at the edge of the landing. All three were less than six feet from the Warrior.

"What do we do, sir?" the tallest of the guards inquired nervously.

"You'll get your orders in a moment," Thayer replied, then smiled at Rikki. "I shouldn't be surprised, but I am."

The martial artist did not respond.

"What happened to my men downstairs?" Thayer inquired.

"They have passed on to the next realm."

"They're dead?"

Rikki nodded.

General Thayer sighed. "The King sent me to escort you upstairs. He wants to see you again."

"And I want to see him. But first, my katana," Rikki stated, extending his right arm.

"You know I can't give it to you. I'd like to, but my duty is to the King."

"Duty should be measured by wisdom and guided by the Spirit."

General Thayer looked sad. "I'm sorry. I truly am."

"So am I," Rikki responded.

Thayer glanced at the two Hounds. "Kill him."

CHAPTER FIFTEEN

The leader of the Hound patrol was a lean sergeant with sandy hair and an arrogant attitude. He sneered at the quartet in front of him and crossed his arms on his chest. Strapped around his narrow waist were a pair of Smith and Wesson Model 459's. "Well, well, well," he declared sarcastically. "What have we here?"

Behind the noncom were five Hounds, each armed with an automatic rifle.

"Howdy," Hickok said, the M-16 held loosely in his right hand.

"Howdy, my ass," the sergeant responded. He studied the blond man in the buckskins and the little girl, then shifted his attention to the giant and the brunette beyond them. "You're the ones!" he exclaimed.

"We are?" Hickok replied.

"You're the ones the platoon was sent after," the sergeant stated. "They must have missed you."

"Nope. They found us," Hickok said.

The Hound sergeant scanned the street. "Then where are they?"

"They're buzzard bait," Hickok answered.

"What?"

Hickok slowly raised his left hand and slashed his forefinger across his neck. As he did, at the moment every Hound was watching his left hand, he surreptitiously tilted the M-16 barrel with his right and squeezed the trigger.

The Hounds were caught napping.

A stunned expression was on the sergeant's face as he was struck in the chest, the slugs stitching his torso from his navel to his right shoulder. His arms flung out as he was smashed onto his back by the impact.

With only his right hand on the blasting, bucking rifle, Hickok could not fully control his aim. The barrel swiveled to the right, the M-16 sending rounds into two of the thunderstruck Hounds, perforating their chests and slamming them to the ground.

Three Hounds were still erect, and they sighted on the gunman and little girl even as their companions died.

Someone else fired before the Hounds could, adding the din of her AR-15 to Hickok's M-16. Bonnie held the stock pressed to her shoulders, and her lips were a grim line as she aimed carefully and fired. Although not an expert markswoman, at a range of 30 feet she could hardly miss. Her shots smacked into the Hounds below their necks, dotting each man's upper chest with crimson holes.

The three Hounds toppled in a tidy row.

Hickok ceased firing and walked to the sergeant. He nudged the body with his right toe. "Cocky bunch of turkeys," he commented.

Shocked by the abrupt violence, Chastity ran to the gunman and grabbed his left leg. "Are these the bad men who took Uncle Rikki?"

"Some of them, princess," Hickok replied.

"Will we find Uncle Rikki soon? I don't like this place."

"The folks hereabouts *are* a mite inhospitable," Hickok said.

"What?"

"These cow chips are real meanies," Hickok clarified.

"They sure are," Chastity agreed.

Blade and Bonnie joined them. Blade knelt and started removing the sergeant's belt and holstered 459's.

"Thanks for the assist, ma'am," Hickok said to Bonnie.

"Don't mention it," Bonnie responded.

"More Hounds will arrive soon," Blade declared, and looked at Bonnie. "You've lived here for a long time. Where can we hide for an hour?"

"We could mingle with the crowds downtown," she proposed. "The Hounds will conduct a thorough search once they find these bodies, but they might not expect us to go there."

"Lead the way," Blade instructed her, rising with the confiscated belt in his left hand.

Bonnie hurried off.

"What about Rikki?" Hickok inquired.

Blade headed after Bonnie. "We won't do him any good if we get caught. We'll lay low for an hour or so, then go get him."

"Now you're talkin," Hickok said.

Bonnie led them on a winding, circuitous route into the inner city. Memphis became even filthier and ever more squalid the farther they went.

"Rats must vacation here," Hickok cracked at one point.

They traversed an alley, darted across a narrow street, and paused under a rusted fire escape.

"In two or three blocks there will be shanties," Bonnie detailed. "Ignore the beggars if you don't want to attract attention."

"Do you have a house of your own?" Blade inquired.

"Clyde and I shared a room in the back of a demolished store on the west side. It was cramped, and there weren't any windows, but the door was sturdy and the lock worked."

"Do all the people in Memphis live under such conditions?" Blade asked.

"Most," Bonnie divulged. "Except for the Hounds. They live in their Headquarters Complex, and everyone should have it so cushy. Anything the Hounds need, they get. They seized all the paint and building supplies they could uncover when they turned the old Depot into the Complex. They confiscated most of the vehicles. And they searched high and low for the material for their uniforms.'' She paused. ''Only one person in Memphis lives better than the Hounds. The King. That bastard has an estate you wouldn't believe. Every time the Hounds raid a town or outpost, the King takes the best of the spoils. He's filthy rich.''

''Let me ask you something,'' Blade said thoughtfully. ''Where would the Hounds bring a prisoner? To the Complex or the King's estate?''

''To the estate,'' Bonnie answered without hesitation. ''The King likes to interrogate prisoners personally.''

''You know this for a fact?''

''My former squeeze, Jeff, told me,'' Bonnie stated.

''Then we should head for the estate,'' Blade declared.

''The King's estate is guarded better than the Complex,'' Bonnie noted. ''You'll never sneak in there.''

''You let us worry about that problem,'' Blade said. ''For now, we'll stroll around downtown Memphis. The Hounds might be expecting an attack at the estate or the Complex. If we delay a bit, they'll slack off and make our job easier.'' He nodded directly ahead. ''Lead the way. You can give us a guided tour of the inner city.''

''We could run into trouble,'' Bonnie predicted.

''Nothin' I can't handle,'' Hickok said.

Bonnie shrugged and walked to the end of the block, then took a left. At the next intersection she turned right, then traveled two blocks. Voices arose, a jumble of conversations, men and women talking and laughing, children playing.

Blade quickly looped the sergeant's gunbelt around his waist above his own belt and fastened the buckle. He aligned the holsters just behind his Bowies, and looked up as they rounded a corner.

The avenue they were entering was packed with people, most of whom were grungy and wore attire in need of repair. Pedestrians crammed the thoroughfare, while on the sidewalks were dozens of booths where shady characters hawked everything under the sun. Haggling and arguments were commonplace.

"Wow!" Chastity exclaimed. "Look at all of them."

"You stay close to me," Hickok advised, slinging the M-16 over his right shoulder and taking her hand in his.

A few of the milling crowd gazed at the newcomers, but the majority went about their business.

"I'll stick out like a sore thumb," Hickok remarked.

"I see other men in buckskins," Blade mentioned, surveying the populace. "Why will you appear any different than them?"

"I took a bath yesterday."

Blade stepped alongside Bonnie. The four of them strolled along the avenue observing the swirl of humanity, alert for Hounds. "I didn't realize there were so many people in Memphis," Blade commented. "Where did they all come from?"

"From all over the Outlands," Bonnie answered. "A lot have arrived in the past month or so, and I've heard that many more are on the way."

"Why would they come here?" Blade queried. "Memphis doesn't have a lot to recommend it."

"Memphis has the Hounds," Bonnie said, "and most of the men arriving here hope to become Hounds. A lot of the people are related to Hounds. Some come because living in the city beats living in the woods. Others want to get in on the ground floor. They expect Memphis to grow like crazy as the Hounds conquer more and more territory."

"How much territory do the Hounds intend to conquer?" Blade asked idly.

"The whole world."

Blade began laughing, but ceased when he realized she was serious. "The Hounds plan to conquer the world?"

"The King does. He told me so himself when he invited me over for a candlelit, romantic supper three nights ago," Bonnie said bitterly.

Blade remembered her earlier comment and put two and two together. "There's no need to go into that, if you don't want—"

"I want to tell you," Bonnie said, cutting him off. "I want you to know the kind of bastard you're dealing with."

"I can imagine," Blade assured her.

Bonnie glanced over her right shoulder at Hickok and Chastity, who were ambling eight feet away. She stared straight ahead somberly. "I never thought it would happen to me."

Blade did not respond.

"I mean, I heard all the tales floating around," Bonnie said softly. "I heard that every month or so the King would have the Hounds scour the city for a bed partner, but I never expected I would be picked."

"There's really no need to discuss this," Blade reiterated.

"Please, let me finish," Bonnie requested. "I have to get this off of my chest. I've told no one the full story." She paused. "I couldn't even bring myself to confide completely in Clyde. I told him bits and pieces, but I knew he'd go off the deep end if I gave him every little detail. I didn't want him storming to the estate and getting murdered by those sons of bitches."

"The Hounds took you to the King?"

"Yeah. I was on my way home with a few strips of venison jerky I'd traded for, when this Hound patrol stopped me and I was ordered to go with them."

"What do you do?"

"At first, I didn't know what was going on. The captain in charge was a tight-lipped scumbag. I didn't catch on until we were near the King's mansion."

"Did you resist?"

"Damn right I did, once I saw where they were taking me. I screamed and demanded to be let go, but the captain had me carried the rest of the way. I'd never met the King, and I wasn't about to let the prick paw all over me," Bonnie detailed. "But before I knew it, there I was in the King's mansion."

"Did they tie you up?"

"No," Bonnie answered. "They didn't need to tie me. There were six guards on the front steps, and I saw other Hounds on the estate and in the mansion. There was nowhere I could go."

"Were you locked in the King's bedroom?" Blade questioned.

"No. Nothing like that. The captain left me inside the front door. I was waiting there, nervous as all hell, when the King came down the stairs. Man, was he something, all decked out in a black uniform with gold buttons and braid, and enough medals to gag a horse. He was all smiles and polite as could be. I told him that I didn't want to be there, that there must be some mistake."

"What did he say?"

"The bastard was slick as shit. He apologized for his men, then invited me to stay for supper. Claimed it was the least he could do," Bonnie said, and frowned. "I should have said no right then, but he was so nice, so—charming—I was sucked right into his trap. I agreed to stay for supper."

"What happened then?"

"The King took me on a personal tour of his mansion. Blade, I never imagined such wealth existed. He has fancy furniture, carpets thicker than grass, paintings and drapes and even a damn chandelier. And his throne room! The man has a gold-plated throne! I've got to admit it. I was really impressed."

"Did you like him?"

Bonnie scowled. "Yeah. I hate to say it, but yeah, I found the creep fascinating. I'd always imagined he was some kind of monster. Little did I know." She closed her eyes for a second and shuddered.

"There's no need to go on," Blade mentioned.

Bonnie ignored him. "So he walked me to his royal dining

room, as he called it, treating me like the perfect lady all the while. You should have seen the spread! A polished table as long as a truck was covered with enough food to feed an army. Meats. Fresh fruit and vegetables. Bread and cakes. And candy bars too. Candy bars! Do you have any idea how rare candy bars are?''

"No," Blade admitted.

"The sucker had a box of them," Bonnie declared in astonishment. "My tummy was doing flip-flops just looking at the table. I probably drooled like a starving dog."

"So you ate your fill?"

"I ate until I was ready to puke," Bonnie responded. "I never knew I could cram so much food into my stomach. And the King talked on and on the whole time, about his big plan to conquer the country, then the world. Something about a vision he had once. Everyone will worship him one day, or some such nonsense. I hardly paid attention, I was so busy stuffing food into my mouth. I topped the meal off with four candy bars. Four." She grinned at the memory.

"And then?"

"And then the meal turned ugly," Bonnie disclosed. "The King had his butler bring a bottle of wine. A vintage year, he said. The King poured my glass himself. I should have suspected something was up. What a jerk I was!"

"You can't blame yourself."

"Who the hell else can I blame? When your mind knows a situation is bad, and your intuition tells you a situation is bad, and you allow yourself to be drawn into it anyway, then there's no one to blame but yourself if you get burnt. True?"

"True," Blade concurred.

"Where was I? Oh, yeah. The wine. About ten minutes after my first glass, I started seeing double and feeling all woozy. I couldn't sit up straight."

"The wine was drugged," Blade decided.

"You got it," Bonnie said. "I heard the King laughing like a lunatic, and then I passed out. When I came to, I was naked and tied to the post of a big canopy bed."

Blade's features hardened. "He stripped you and bound you to his bed?"

Bonnie nodded, her lips trembling. "That was only the beginning. The next thing I know, the King waltzes into the room. But get this. The man was wearing lacy undies, mesh stockings, and carrying a whip."

"A whip?"

"Yeah. One of those leather whips with the round handles."

"You can stop right there," Blade said. "I get the picture."

Bonnie sighed and her eyes watered. "He did sick things to me, Blade. Gross things. Do you want me to pull my shirt up and show you the marks? I'll prove it to you."

"No," Blade replied softly.

"I can't sleep anymore," Bonnie went on. "Every time I close my eyes, I see his face leering at me and feel his teeth. The bastard gave me gold coins, but I tossed them in his face."

"There is more to be done here than rescuing Rikki," Blade commented harshly.

"What do you mean?"

"I'm going to terminate the King."

"Terminate?" Bonnie repeated, and halted. She looked into his simmering gray eyes. "You intend to kill the King?"

Blade nodded.

"Now wait a minute," Bonnie said. "I never meant to involve you in my affairs—"

"It's not just your affair," Blade replied. "The Hounds ambushed us and abducted Rikki. The King is their leader, so the King will pay the price."

Bonnie shook her head. "You don't know what you're saying. I agreed to help you because I want to do whatever I can to hurt the bastard, and freeing your friend should piss him off no end. But trying to kill the King is a whole new game. We can't do it by ourselves."

"We intended to free Rikki by ourselves," Blade noted.

"That's different. That's a matter of locating where they're holding him and setting him free. But killing the King means you have to go up against all of the Hounds and the Dark Lord. There's no way we could win."

"What is this Dark Lord?"

"I've never seen him, but I've heard all the stories. The Dark Lord does the dirty work for the King. Some people say the Dark Lord is a mutant."

"I've fought mutants before," Blade said.

"This isn't your fight," Bonnie stated.

"You're wrong," Blade responded. "This became our fight the moment the Hounds attacked us."

"You'd be better off if you found your friend and left Memphis," Bonnie said. "You're just asking for trouble if you try to kill the King."

Blade scratched his chin. "In other words, we should avoid a confrontation instead of dealing with the problem?"

"Yeah."

"You sound like one of the prewar types," Blade remarked.

"The what?"

Blade idly gazed at a cloud overhead. "We study the prewar society in depth at our Home during our schooling years. Our Elders wanted us to recognize the flaws in the prewar culture so we won't commit the same mistakes. The prewar society prided itself on being a nation of laws. They forgot that they were a nation of people, and they allowed their laws to replace the development of genuine character."

"I don't understand," Bonnie declared.

"Let me put it this way," Blade said. "What would you do if a guy came up to you and slapped you on the face?"

"Kick him in the balls."

Blade smirked. "Well, in the prewar society, they believed in settling every problem through the law. If someone was attacked, they were supposed to do the civilized thing and sue the attacking party. Personal retribution was taboo. The liberal leaders, the social scientists and the psychologists, used the educational institutions and the media to turn the people into spineless jelly—into wimps, as Hickok would say. We have literature in our library from the period. The books actually encourage women not to resist if someone tries to rape them, and advise men to do nothing if someone should break into their home in the middle of the night. Gun owners were branded as barbaric morons. If a man or woman did defend themselves against assailants, *they* were taken to court by the government.''

"I don't get it. Why would the leaders do such a thing to the people?''

"Because you can lead a cow easier than a bull," Blade replied. "The forefathers of America were rugged, independent men who believed in individual liberty and the right to bear arms. But the leaders of America at the time of the war were pampered power-mongers who tried to mold the people in the image of their own narrow minds. To them, the law was everything. To them, group rights took priority over individual rights.''

"What does all of this have to do with the King?''

"We all must take responsibility for the evil we encounter in our lives. We can't run away from it, or bury our heads in the sand and hope it will go away. The people in the prewar society never dealt with evil head-on. They tried to control evil by passing hundreds of thousands of laws outlawing evil behavior. But evil can't be controlled by words printed on paper. Evil must be eradicated at the source.'' Blade paused, pondering. "The King is the source of the evil growing in Memphis, and if he isn't stopped now, the evil will spread. I have a responsibility to insure the evil does not go any further.''

"You could wind up dead.''

"And how many untold thousands will wind up dead if the King isn't stopped?''

Bonnie stared at him in admiration. "I wish I had your courage.''

"You do.''

She snorted. "If I had your courage, I would have taken care of the King the other night. But I didn't."

"You were never given the opportunity," Blade said. "You should be grateful you survived. I'm surprised the King didn't have you killed."

"I expected him to kill me," Bonnie admitted. "But he made a big production out of sparing my life. He said I might be carrying his seed, and I should be grateful for the chance to participate in the spread of his glory, whatever the hell that meant." She placed her left hand on her abdomen. "If I end up pregnant with his kid, I'll shoot myself."

"Has he done this to others?"

"From what I hear, he does it about every other month or so. Sometimes with men, sometimes with women. I also heard he likes children on occasion."

"Children?"

"He'd probably use dogs if he could catch them."

Blade opened his mouth to speak, when a harsh outburst to his rear caused him to spin, his hands dropping to his Bowies.

Four hardcases were shoving their way through the crowd, led by a tall barrel of a man dressed in rough animal hides and sporting a silver nose ring. They were coming up behind Hickok and Chastity, and the gunman was slowing and glancing over his left shoulder.

"Out of my way!" bellowed Nose Ring, and gave the gunfighter and the girl a shove.

CHAPTER SIXTEEN

The pair of Hounds reacted to General Thayer's order to kill the Warrior according to their training; predictably, they attempted to unsling their AR-15's.

Rikki-Tikki-Tavi was already in motion. He wanted to dispatch the duo and retrieve his katana from the Spartan expeditiously and quietly. Any shots would undoubtedly draw more Hounds to the scene. He needed to render the pair unconscious before they could fire, and accordingly he sprang forward as they began to unsling their rifles, releasing the AR-15 he was carrying. He took two strides and leaped into the air, his fists clenched in the Oriental manner, his right leg tucked tight, his left extended.

"Look ou—" the Hound on the right started to yell.

Rikki's left foot connected with the Hound's sternum and sent the man sailing backwards to crash into the general. The Warrior landed lightly as the officer and the private tumbled down the stairs in a tangle of arms and legs.

To the left the second guard was trying to level his AR-15.

Rikki pivoted, sliding in toward the Hound, shifting his balance onto his left leg and cocking his right at a 45-degree angle. He executed a side-thrust kick, using his thigh to maximize the power in his blow, twisting at the waist as he made contact.

The second Hound was struck in the ribs. There was a

distinct crack and he doubled over, dropping his rifle.

With his right hand clenched in the Tettsui, the iron-hammer fist, Rikki smashed the Hound on the right temple.

Uttering a nasal wheeze, the man sprawled onto the floor.

Eight steps below, the general and the private were in the act of disengaging and getting to their feet. Thayer was on his knees, his right hand on the katana hilt. The Hound had lost his AR-15, which had clattered several steps lower.

Rikki took the stairs three at a time. His second spring brought him to the rising guard, his right knee flicking as he kicked the private full in the face.

The Hound went flying, crunching onto his head six steps below and lying still.

Rikki came down on his toes two steps lower than the Spartan. He whirled.

"I always said you were good," General Thayer remarked. He stood in a crouch, the katana clenched in his brawny hands.

"I want my katana," Rikki said.

"I intend to give it to you," Thayer replied, grinning. "Edge first."

Rikki assumed the Fudo-tachi, the ready stance. "I have no desire to harm you."

"You're putting the cart before the horse," Thayer responded. "I said you were good. I'm better."

"This will prove nothing."

"Not for you maybe."

"You can leave in peace."

General Thayer's lips curled downward. "What is this? Sympathy?"

"Call it the respect due one warrior from another," Rikki said.

Thayer smiled. "I appreciate the compliment. I wish we had met under different circumstances."

"I feel the same way," Rikki acknowledged.

The Spartan shrugged. "Such is life."

"We don't need to do this," Rikki stressed.

"I'm afraid we do."

"Is dying for a madman a fitting rite of passage for men such as us?" Rikki inquired.

"I have my duty."

"And I have mine."

General Thayer straightened. "Then there's nothing more to be said."

"I guess not," Rikki said with a tinge of melancholy in his tone.

Thayer bowed slightly. "I salute you," he stated, and as he rose he slashed viciously at the Warrior's neck.

Almost taken unawares, Rikki barely evaded the swipe of the gleaming sword. He wrenched his body backwards and saw the blade come within a hair's-breath of his throat, then allowed his momentum to carry him from the step. On the stairs the Spartan had the advantage. Rikki wanted room to maneuver, to employ his legs. He landed two steps lower, and without breaking stride vaulted even lower.

General Thayer was determined not to be denied. He dashed after the bounding Warrior, swinging the katana again and again, repeatedly missing by less than an inch. His left foot slipped on an object blocking one of the steps, and he looked down in time to avoid tripping over the corpse of the private with the split skull.

Rikki gained a few feet on his pursuer, covering four steps at a leap and reaching the bottom of the stairs in three jumps. He raced along the corridor, searching for anything he could utilize as a weapon.

General Thayer was hot on the Warrior's heels.

Midway along the hall Rikki risked a glance over his right shoulder. The Spartan was six feet behind him, the katana spearing toward his back. His facile mind instantaneously recognized an unorthodox opening, and with the recognition came simultaneous execution. He abruptly dropped, flattening on the tile, his body across the hall, resting on his hands and toes.

The Spartan was unable to check his headlong advance.

His boots caught on the Warrior's form and he lost his balance, toppling over, deliberately adding to the force of the fall by hurling himself even farther, putting more distance between them.

Rikki had expected to rise swiftly and render Thayer unconscious while the Spartan was sprawled on the floor. Instead, he saw the officer slide and roll and heave erect before he could reach him.

Thayer held the katana at the ready position and grinned. "Nice move. You almost had me."

"It would have sufficed for most."

"I told you I was trained by the best. Spartans are bred for combat."

"So are Warriors."

General Thayer cocked his head and studied his adversary. "You say that word as if it's a title of some kind."

"It is."

The Spartan's eyes widened. "The Warriors! Of course!"

"You've heard of us?" Rikki asked.

"Yes," Thayer said. "But I never made the connection until right now. Four or five years ago everyone was talking about the defeat of the Civilized Zone at the hands of a small band of fighters called Warriors. You're one of them?"

"I am."

"I should have realized the Warriors were involved in the Leather Knight incident. It explains a lot."

"You've heard of us," Rikki observed. "Why is it that we've never heard of the Spartans?"

"They like to keep to themselves. Sparta was built shortly after the war in an isolated valley by a survivalist with a penchant for Spartan history."

"Where is the valley located?"

"There you go again," General Thayer muttered. "Enough talk, Warrior. Let's finish this."

"Must we?"

"Yes," Thayer hissed, and lunged, swinging the katana at the Warrior's head.

Rikki backpedaled, then sidestepped as the Spartan tried to impale his stomach. He delivered a palm-heel thrust to the Spartan's body above the spleen.

Thayer grunted and retreated several steps, keeping his back to the opposite wall.

Still seeking room to maneuver, Rikki ran down the corridor toward the cell at the end, the same cell he'd vacated a short while ago. He saw the open cell door and the two bodies on the floor, and he also saw a pistol strapped around one of the prone pair.

General Thayer was pounding in pursuit.

Rikki poured on the speed, and when he arrived at the cell he had a five-yard lead. In a flash he was at the Hound's side, drawing the pistol from the holster and whirling.

Thayer halted in the doorway, both hands on the katana, both eyes on the pistol.

"Don't even think it," Rikki said.

The Spartan hesitated.

"Place my katana at your feet," Rikki directed.

General Thayer frowned as he lowered the sword to the floor.

"Step back," Rikki instructed, wagging the pistol. "Away from the katana."

Thayer reluctantly complied, taking four giant strides, his arms in the air.

Rikki walked to the katana and looked down at his cherished blade.

"Finish me!" General Thayer snapped.

"Are you in a hurry to die?" Rikki inquired, looking up.

"I have failed Aloysius, just as I failed my king in Sparta," Thayer said. "My disgrace has been doubly compounded. Finish me and end my misery."

"I will not shoot you in cold blood."

"And I will not allow you to pass me alive," Thayer declared.

Rikki peered at the Spartan for several seconds, gazed at his katana, then glanced at the pistol in his right hand. He deposited the pistol alongside the katana.

Thayer's mouth slackened. "What—?"

Straightening, Rikki adopted the cat stance.

Profound amazement rippled across the Spartan's visage. "Do you know what you're doing?"

"Whenever you are ready," Rikki said.

The general's brow knit in confusion. "Why?" he asked plaintively.

Rikki's belated response was laconic, yet eloquently precise. "Because we are who we are."

Thayer nodded slowly, then dropped into the horse stance. "I should warn you. Spartans are taught martial combat before they are weaned."

"Really?" Rikki responded with a grin. "Warriors are instructed in the martial arts in the womb. We save time that way."

A hearty laugh burst from the Spartan's lips. He raised his hands and slid forward. "I shall regret slaying you, and I've never regretted killing anyone before."

"Now who is putting the cart before the horse?"

Thayer closed cautiously, and when he was within a yard of the Warrior he unleashed a flurry of hand and foot strikes, any one of which would have incapacitated an ordinary adversary.

Rikki-Tikki-Tavi was not ordinary. He blocked and adroitly countered every blow, holding his ground, his stoic expression inscrutable, displaying his supreme mastery of diverse forms and styles. Karate. Kung Fu. Aikido. Judo. Jujitsu. He never gave an inch, withstanding the Spartan's onslaught as immovably as a firmly rooted tree would resist a raging storm.

Sweat was beading Thayer's brow when he unexpectedly stepped back and smiled. "This won't be as easy as I thought."

Rikki slid forward in a low stance, his hands and arms resembling cranes poised to smite a fish.

General Thayer inched to the rear, maintaining a defensive

posture, his eyes narrowing.

To disconcert his opponent, Rikki shifted from the crane to the tiger form, from the tiger to the dragon, and from the dragon to the snake, each movement fluid and balletic. He was two feet from his taller foe, waiting for an opening to present itself. As he glided his right foot closer to the Spartan, Thayer committed a blunder.

The general attempted to snap-kick the Warrior's right knee.

Rikki easily moved his right leg to the left, and as Thayer's boot cleaved the air, he struck, aiming a leopard-paw blow at the officer's midsection. Thayer deflected Rikki's arm with an outside circling block, then drove his right fist at the Warrior's solar plexus. Rikki's right arm flashed in a cutting forearm block, his feet shifting to the right as he performed a horizontal elbow strike to Thayer's chest.

Staggered by the jarring pain, Thayer inadvertently stumbled backwards, then recovered promptly.

Rikki came again.

Thayer, resolved to stand firm, met the Warrior head-on.

Minutes elapsed.

The corridor was filled with the muted smacks, cuffs, and thumps of their rain of blows. Their shadows seemed to be entwined in a macabre dance on the walls. Hands and feet clashed, countered, and clashed again. The progress of their combat drew them farther and farther from the cell, until they were within three yards of the stairs once more.

Rikki sustained two agonizing hits, one to the left side of his neck, the other to his right leg below the knee.

Hoping to put an end to the conflict, and annoyed at himself for not killing the Warrior sooner, Thayer became less careful as he pressed the Warrior. He glowered as he fought, his ferocity mounting.

Rikki counterstruck every blow, operating on sheer instinct, his arms and legs functioning in an automatic, conditioned reflex, the result of years spent honing his skills in practice and in battle. During the course of their savage

exchange, he landed four blows to the Spartan's nerve centers
and vital points, yet Thayer managed to shrug off every one
and continue fighting. They appeared to be evenly matched,
and the outcome was in definite doubt. Rikki slowed slightly,
hoping to convey the misimpression he was tiring.

Thayer took the bait. Sensing victory, he slashed his right
hand at the Warrior's neck, but had to settle for a glancing
blow off Rikki's collarbone as the wiry martial artist leaned
back.

At that moment, as the officer's right arm was extended
to the side, Rikki knifed his right hand up and in, his fingers
rigid as steel, into Thayer's ribs. The Spartan gasped and
tried to escape to the rear, but Rikki was on him with the
speed of a swooping eagle. The Warrior's right hand arced
into Thayer's cardiac notch, the area below the left breast,
sinking in to the knuckles.

General Thayer grunted and stiffened. He tottered backwards, his features contorted in overwhelming torment. With
an effort, he focused on the Warrior, and his look of anguish
was replaced by shocked consternation. Shaking his head,
his lips moving noiselessly, he sank to his knees.

Rikki-Tikki-Tavi draped his arms at his sides and bowed.
A frown curled his mouth as he straightened, and he inhaled
deeply before speaking. "You *were* one of the best I've
encountered."

Thayer appeared to be on the verge of tears. He nodded
once, then croaked four words. "Tell the Spartans I . . ."

Rikki saw the life flicker from the officer's eyes, and he
watched in silence as Thayer sank to the tile. For over a
minute he stared at Thayer's face, and his voice was un-
characteristically choked with emotion when he finally
responded. "I will tell them," he promised.

Footsteps sounded at the top of the stairs.

Rikki spun and retraced his steps to the cell. He leaned
over and reclaimed his katana, then turned.

A sole Hound was descending the last few steps, his startled
gaze on the general's body. He was armed with a pistol in

a flapped holster on his right hip, and he reached for the gun as he saw the small man in black rushing toward him.

"You killed them—" the Hound blurted out.

Rikki was on the man as the pistol was being leveled. His katana whipped in a glistening swing, the razor edge cleaving the Hound's wrist before the trigger finger could tighten on the trigger. The private opened his mouth to scream, but the best he could do was gurgle as the katana slit his throat from ear to ear. Blood spurted everywhere. The Hound reeled toward the stairs, collapsing after two paces. Rikki walked past him, beginning to climb the steps. He looked back once at the Hound's stupefied visage.

"Never belabor the obvious."

CHAPTER SEVENTEEN

Chastity lost her grip on Hickok's hand and fell on her buttocks. "Daddy!" she cried.

Nose Ring and his companions laughed as they brushed past the gunman, but they only took one step before his enraged voice stopped them in their tracks.

"That's far enough!"

The hardcases turned slowly, confident in themselves, smirking. All four wore handguns. All four radiated a palpable air of menace.

"Where the hell do you think you're going?" Hickok demanded, his hands hovering next to his Pythons.

"What's it to you?" Nose Ring replied contemptuously. He saw a woman with an automatic rifle come around and pick up the blonde girl.

Hickok glanced at Chastity and Bonnie, then, incredibly, hooked his thumbs in his gunbelt and grinned. "What a wit. You must be the brains in your family."

Nose Ring bristled. "I wouldn't push it, if I were you."

"Thank the Spirit you're not me," Hickok mocked him. "I wouldn't want to look that ugly and smell that bad if I could help it."

"Do you know who you're talking to?"

"Four medical marvels."

"What?"

"Four livin', breathin' dead men."

Nose Ring looked at the other hardcases. "We're not dead yet."

The nearest pedestrians were discreetly trying to put as much distance as they could between themselves and the altercation.

"You can count the minutes you have left on one hand," Hickok declared.

Nose Ring scrutinized the guy in the buckskins, noting the pearl-handled revolvers and the M-16 over the guy's left shoulder. He experienced a fleeting sensation of dread, but shook it off by thinking of all the saps he'd wasted in his travels. No one had ever beaten him, and no one ever would.

"We don't want any trouble," said someone to their rear.

The four hardcases looked behind them to find a giant in a black leather vest.

"You don't want any trouble?" Nose Ring repeated.

"No," the giant stated, looking at the guy in buckskins. "We don't want to get in trouble with the Hounds, do we?"

"Did you see what these cow chips did?" Hickok demanded.

"I saw," Blade said.

"Are you sayin' I can't teach them manners?"

"We don't want to attract the Hounds," Blade reiterated.

"Nobody treats Chastity that way," Hickok remarked angrily.

"We don't want trouble," Blade said yet again.

"What's the big deal?" Nose Ring interjected. "So what if the little cunt got knocked on her ass?"

Blade sighed and put his hands on his hips. "Did you eat radioactive waste when you were younger?"

"What kind of dumb-ass question is that?" Nose Ring rejoined.

"I just thought there might be a logical explanation for your suicide complex," Blade said.

"Suicide?" Nose Ring snorted. "I don't want to kill myself, you jerk."

Blade walked to the left, out of the line of fire, and grinned. "You just did, you jerk."

"I'll make this fair," Hickok declared. "You can go for your irons first."

"Do you think you can take all four of us?" Nose Ring demanded.

"In my sleep."

Nose Ring gazed at each of the other hardcases, then chuckled. "Let's show this windbag."

Pedestrians were now running in every direction.

"Whenever you coyotes get the notion," Hickok said. "But I don't have all day for you to get up the nerve."

"Screw you!" Nose Ring snapped, and went for his gun, his companions doing likewise.

Hickok seemed to be frozen in place. He stayed immobile as their hands streaked to their handguns, and he was motionless as those handguns began to rise and clear leather. Not until Nose Ring was leveling a revolver did the gunfighter move, his draw a literal blur, both Colts blasting.

Nose Ring and the hardcase to his left were struck in the forehead, and both of them rocked on their heels and toppled over. The last two hardcases fared no better. They were struck down before they could bring their revolvers into play, one shot through the left eye, the other the right.

Hickok stared at the four corpses for a moment. "I wonder how they managed to put on their pants without help," he quipped. Then he started reloading the spent rounds in his Colts.

Blade surveyed the sea of stunned expressions surrounding them. "The Hounds will investigate, won't they?" he asked Bonnie.

"At the most, we have five minutes," she replied.

"Let's get out of here," Blade said.

"Do you still want to lay low for an hour?" Bonnie queried.

"No," Blade answered. "Laying low wouldn't accomplish anything now. Take us directly to the King's estate."

"About time," Hickok interjected. "I'm tired of this pussy-footin' around."

Bonnie headed northward. "Stay close to me." She smiled at Chastity. "Are you okay?"

Snug in Bonnie's arms, Chastity nodded. "My daddy taught *them* a lesson."

"I've never seen anyone as fast as your daddy," Bonnie commented.

Chastity beamed. "Yeah. Daddy is real good at shooting people. He shoots them all the time."

"Remind me to never get your daddy mad at me," Bonnie said.

"I wouldn't let him shoot you," Chastity declared. "I like you."

"Gee, thanks," Bonnie responded.

"Unless you got him real mad," Chastity added. "Then it might be okay for him to shoot you in the foot."

Bonnie grinned. "I'm beginning to understand why the two of you are so close."

"Are we two peas in a pod?"

"Yeah. I'd say so. Where did you hear that?"

"Uncle Rikki said so," Chastity replied.

"I haven't met your Uncle Rikki yet. Is he nice?"

"Real nice. He teases Daddy a lot."

"Does Uncle Rikki have a woman?"

"Yep. A lady named Lexine. She lives at their Home."

"Figures," Bonnie said wistfully.

The Warriors came abreast of them.

"Do you want me to hold you, princess?" Hickok asked.

"I don't mind," Bonnie said.

"I'm fine," Chastity stated. "You'd better be ready in case more bad men show up."

"How many people have you shot?" Bonnie inquired.

"I never counted 'em," Hickok said.

"A few? A lot?"

"What difference does it make?" Hickok retorted.

"I was just curious," Bonnie explained. "Have you ever

shot anyone in the foot?''

"Once or twice. Why?"

"Oh, nothing," Bonnie commented, and laughed.

The gunman looked at Blade. "Why are women so blamed weird?"

"I never noticed they were," Blade replied.

"I keep forgettin'. Your missus has the wool pulled over your eyes," Hickok declared.

"She does not."

"And you don't think that womenfolk are a teensy-weensy bit on the strange side?"

"No."

"I rest my case."

They hurried along the avenue. The farther they went, the less attention was directed their way. After four blocks no one was gawking at them.

Hickok looked over his right shoulder. "Looks like we hood-winked those varmints."

"You spoke too soon," Blade said, nodding to the north.

A Hound patrol was approaching down the middle of the boulevard, pushing through the crowd, the sergeant in the lead barking for everyone to stand aside.

"Quick," Blade declared, angling to the right-hand curb. He halted at a rickety wooden booth manned by a grizzled proprietor with a toothless smirk, who was wearing a bed-raggled wool coat even in the August heat.

"Can I help you?" the man asked. "Honest Ike is my name."

Blade rested his hands on his knees and pretended to inspect the wares in the stand, casually regarding a collection of rusted pots and pans, dog-eared books, faded clothes, various utensils, and assorted odds and ends.

"Everything is ten percent off today," Ike informed them. "I'm having a clearance sale."

"You make a living sellin' this stuff?" Hickok queried, fingering a glass unicorn with three legs and a broken horn.

"Yep. And don't touch the merchandise, sonny. You break it, you pay for it."

"Where do you find this junk?" Hickok asked.

Honest Ike glared at the gunman. "I'll thank you not to call my quality merchandise junk. Folks come from miles around to trade with me."

Blade gazed at the avenue, watching the Hound patrol as they hastened to the south.

"What's that?" Hickok inquired, pointing at a battered paperback in the corner of a shelf. Displayed on the cover was a snarling hound in a gold Egyptian headdress.

"It's a book, dummy."

"I know that," Hickok said. "Is it any good?"

"Why don't you read it and find out."

"How much?"

"For you, I'll let it go for eight bullets."

Hickok glanced at the old-timer. "Eight rounds of ammo for a book?"

"We don't need anything," Blade said, straightening. The Hound patrol was out of sight.

"Seven bullets," Ike said.

"Is it a horror book?" Hickok asked.

"It's a scary one, all right," Ike confirmed. "Lots of blood and gore. It's about this plague—"

"No, thanks," Hickok said.

"Six bullets."

"No," Hickok responded, turning away.

"Five."

"No."

"Why not?"

"I'm partial to Westerns."

"It has sex in it."

Hickok halted and stared at the book. "It does?"

"Forget the book," Blade directed, nudging the gunman's left shoulder. "We have important business to attend to. Remember?"

"A little literary culture never hurt anyone," Hickok remarked.

They resumed their trek in a northerly direction, on the alert for Hounds.

"Say, Daddy?" Chastity spoke up two blocks later.

"What, missy?"

"What did that man mean?"

"About what?"

"That word he used," Chastity said.

"Which word?"

"Sex. What's sex?"

Hickok did a double take. "Sex?" he blurted out.

"What is it?" Chastity inquired earnestly.

"Yeah, Daddy. I'd like to hear this myself. What is sex?" Blade queried impishly.

"Didn't anyone ever tell you about sex?" Hickok asked.

"No."

"She's only six, for crying out loud," Blade noted.

"How about the birds and the bees?" Hickok questioned.

"I know about them," Chastity said. "Birds have feathers and wings and fly. Bees have wings and stingers."

"You sure know your birds and bees," Hickok muttered.

"So what's sex?" Chastity persisted inquisitively.

"Uhhhh," Hickok stalled, keenly conscious of the amused gazes of Blade and Bonnie. "Sex is what happens when a man's hormones are all agitated and a woman is feelin' generous."

"I don't get it."

"Have you ever noticed that men and women are different?"

"Yep," Chastity responded.

"You have?"

"Women are smarter."

"Says who?"

"My mom said that all the time."

"Do you know about kissin'?"

Chastity scrunched her nose. "Kissing is yucky stuff."

"You'll like it better when you grow up."

"Never," Chastity declared. "I've seen people kissing and hugging. Once I saw this guy and girl in the park, and they were kissing and hugging and wrestling all at the same time."

"Well, I'll tell you what," Hickok said. "When you finally decide that kissin' isn't yucky, you should ask your new mommy about sex."

"Will she know?"

"She's a fair hand at it," Hickok acknowledged.

"I'll ask my new mommy when we get to the Home," Chastity promised. "And I'll ask her why she's fair at it."

"Uh-oh," Hickok said.

Laughing quietly, Bonnie looked at Blade. "Does he always stick his foot in his mouth?"

"Only when his mouth is open," Blade replied.

They traveled another three blocks without incident.

"We take a right," Bonnie instructed as they neared an intersection.

"How far to the estate?" Blade asked.

"Three miles, give or take," Bonnie told him.

They bore to the right along a narrow street. Few of the barter booths were in evidence, and the number of pedestrians had dwindled.

"We'll make better time," Bonnie said.

Although they were able to increase their speed without arousing any undue glances or suspicion, Blade chafed at the pace. He was eager to locate Rikki and leave Memphis far behind. All he could think of was the stashed jeep and the likelihood of being with his loved ones in another week. After such a prolonged separation, such a reaction was natural.

And costly.

Engrossed in his reflection, Blade was not devoting his full attention to the road and sidewalks. His acute hearing vaguely registered a jumble of subdued noises from a junction ahead, but he was absently wondering if they would be able to rescue Rikki before nightfall.

"Take a left," Bonnie mentioned.

"Are your arms gettin' tired?" Hickok inquired.

Bonnie glanced at the gunman and smiled. "No. But thanks. I can carry her for a mile yet."

They started to round the corner.

"You won't need to carry the child that far, my dear," stated someone arrogantly. "We wouldn't want you to strain yourself."

"You!" Bonnie exclaimed in horror.

A lone figure stood in the center of the street 20 feet away, his hands clasped behind his back. He wore a black uniform glittering with gold medals. His hair, mustache, and beard were all black. "Yes, vixen. It is I." He raised his right hand and snapped his fingers. "But I didn't come alone."

Dozens of Hounds materialized, training their weapons on the Warriors and the woman. They were stationed on the rooftops and positioned at upper-story windows. They poured from doorways, forming two rows across the street behind the man with the medals. A pair of jeeps roared from an alley farther down and raced almost to the two rows before braking. A Hound stood in the rear of each vehicle, manning a swivel-mounted machine gun.

"Have you missed me, Bonnie?" the man said with a sneer.

Bonnie uttered a plaintive groan. "We're dead!"

CHAPTER EIGHTEEN

Rikki-Tikki-Tavi glided up the stairs with pantherish finesse, reaching the landing door without making a sound, his katana in his right hand. A muted hubbub arose on the far side as he took hold of the doorknob, and he cautiously eased the door open a crack to hear better.

"—every guard except Pierce, Brosnan, and us out front."

"What's going on?"

"I heard he's really pissed off. Something about a platoon being attacked."

"The platoon the general took out this morning?"

"No. Another platoon."

"Two platoons in one day? You're kidding."

"Hey, I only know what I was told, and I th . . ."

The voices tapered off as the speakers hurried out of range. What was this? Were the guards assembling at the front of the mansion? If so, why? And if they were, this might be the opportunity he needed. Rikki widened the opening until he could slip through, pausing in the corridor to orient himself. If he remembered correctly, going to the right would take him in the general direction of the stairs to the second floor and the throne room. He padded stealthily to another hall, taking the right-hand fork, his ears primed to catch the faintest sound.

The next corridor was reached uneventfully.

Where were all the guards? Outside?

Rikki took a left, and he was 20 feet into the hallway when a scarcely audible conversation wafted from up ahead, growing louder with each second.

Hounds!

He spotted a door to his left and raced over. A quick check insured it wasn't locked, and he was inside, his left ear pressed to the panel, in an instant. He found himself in a storage closet filled with mops, brooms, and cleaning supplies. The light came through a narrow window high on the rear wall.

"—want to be in the general's shoes when the King gets back."

"He ordered me to haul my ass down to the holding cells and find out what's keeping General Thayer. He sounded mad as hell. He said something about showing the general how to do his job. And then he took off with the estate guards and two truckloads from the Complex. Also had a couple of jeeps. Looked like he was ready to start a war."

"Did you hear the scuttlebutt about two platoons being wasted?"

"Yeah. And I don't believe it for a minute."

"You don't?"

"Give me a break. Who could wipe out two platoons?"

"The Leather Knights."

"Those suck-egg pansies can't beat their meat without help. They couldn't take on two of our platoons."

Rikki gauged the two men to be several yards past the storage closet door. He opened it, confirming his guess, and stepped into the corridor. The duo might stumble on him later if he spared them. He wanted them out of the way so he could achieve his goal unhindered. Each had an AR-15 slung over a shoulder, but neither were wearing sidearms.

"Excuse me," Rikki said.

The Hounds stopped and glanced back, surprise twisting their features.

"You!" the one on the left exclaimed.

"Would you care to surrender?" Rikki asked.

In response, the guards tried to bring their Ar-15's into play. They were pathetically slow.

To the Warrior, whose speed was uncanny and whose reflexes were honed to seemingly superhuman levels, the pair of Hounds moved with all the quickness of solidified lava. He was on them before either could completely unsling his rifle, his katana flashing, cleaving the forehead of the guard on the right, then slicing the neck of the other Hound.

They died horribly, whining and gurgling and convulsing on the floor, geysers of blood spattering onto the floor and the walls, both terrified at the prospect of slipping into eternity, and both doing so with a hideous death mask as the legacy to their passing.

Rikki jogged to the end of the hall, took a right, and in 30 seconds was standing in the broad central hallway. He dashed to the stairs and went up them three at a time. A sharp right, and he was running toward the throne room. He doubted the King would permit anyone to be in the throne room when the royal personage was absent, so he took a calculated gamble by throwing the door open when he arrived and springing inside.

The throne room was empty.

He crossed quickly to the rear door in the right-hand wall, hesitating before turning the knob, mentally girding himself. If his suspicion was correct, entering the Dark Lord's chamber was the key to unraveling the mystery of Aloysius the First's sway over the people of Memphis. If he was wrong, he'd be up against a mutant endowed with incalculable power.

There was only one way to find out.

Rikki took a deep breath, twisted the doorknob, and shoved. The door swept inward to reveal an inky chamber. He advanced several strides, the katana held in the jodan-no-kamae position, tensed to counter any attack. He waited for the blazing red orbs and the radiant globes to appear, but nothing materialized.

Was his deduction accurate or was the Dark Lord off
somewhere?

He backed to the wall and felt its smooth surface with his
left hand, running his palm from waist height to as high as
his shoulder and down again, moving away from the
doorway. He went eight feet and found what he wanted.

A light switch.

Rikki faced the chamber and flicked the switch.

A series of overhead fluorescent bulbs illuminated the
entire, large chamber, casting the Dark Lord's abode in a
pale, yellowish glow. The floor was composed of green tiles.
Pale white squares of an unknown substance coated the walls
and the ceiling. Dominating the room was a wide stage
situated along the rear wall, and resting on the stage was
the Dark Lord.

Rikki walked forward, marveling at the sight in front of
him.

Positioned at both ends of the stage were enormous
rectangular boxlike affairs, easily six feet tall, consisting of
wooden side panels and a black plastic grill. Complicated
electronic equipment flanked the gigantic boxes. Between
each box and the center of the stage was a tall metal pedestal
supporting a glass sphere. Inside both spheres was a tapered
gray needle. And filling the center of the stage, near the front,
dangled a peculiar glass or plastic panel suspended from the
roof by silver chains. Underneath the panel was a console,
its back to the room, with a microphone on the top.

What did it all mean?

Rikki angled to the left and found a short flight of steps
to the stage. He hastened up, moving past the immense box
and the odd pedestal to the control console. An array of
switches, buttons, and meters evidently operated the equipment. He leaned over the console, studying the labels under
each one, until he spied a white button marked POWER ON.
His left forefinger depressed the button, and the console
began to hum as the meters became lit and other small

indicator lights came on.

Now what?

He found a toggle switch marked GLOBES and thumbed it down.

The glass spheres on the pedestals made a buzzing noise as blue and purple rays shot from the gray needles to the inner surface of the glass, arcing and sparkling.

Rikki stared at the spheres, puzzled. What purpose did they serve? He scanned the console, noting a recessed keyboard near his midriff, and tapped four of the keys. With each tap the chamber reverberated to raucous musical notes thundering from the boxlike objects.

Most strange.

He noticed a button labeled SATAN'S EYES and pressed it with his left index finger. Glancing overhead, he discovered a pair of fiery red eyes had appeared on the panel hanging from the silver chains.

This was mystifying.

Rikki contemplated the purpose for the equipment. The boxlike objects must be colossal speakers. The Family owned a few shortwave radios, and each incorporated a small speaker in its housing. But what about the spheres and the eyes? Were they part of a bizarre light show, a special effect—

Special effect?

He recalled the history of the mansion as disclosed by the King. The noble man in the painting had been the first to own the estate, and then a musical group. Was it possible the equipment on the stage was theirs? Was this chamber their practice room? Did that explain the keyboard and the speakers? He thought of the posters of the outlandish musicians decorating the throne room. Had the last owners of the estate been like those pictured in the posters? If so, everything was explained.

The King must have found this room when he occupied the mansion, and discovered the special effects while tinkering with the console. Perhaps it was then that his insane mind had concocted the scheme of using the equipment to further his mad ambition. What had General Thayer said? There had been dissension in the ranks. A month after moving into the mansion, Aloysius had called a dissatisfied captain into this very room. Thayer and the other Hounds in the throne room had heard a terrible racket—the music from the speakers? And the King had come out with the dead captain.

Rikki stared at the console, immersed in speculation.

Aloysius must have decided to use the equipment to create the illusion of the Dark Lord. The idea was brilliant. What better way to stifle protest and insure obedience than to fabricate a dreaded deity that would punish transgressors with instant death?

The thought caused the Warrior to frown.

Not quite everything was explained.

What about the deaths?

Dozens of victims killed without a trace of violence on their corpses.

How could this have been done?

Some of the victims were found in locked rooms, and Thayer had mentioned one man killed ten miles from Memphis.

If the Dark Lord was a fake, then Aloysius must be responsible for the deaths. But what technique was he employing?

Rikki turned off the power and watched the spheres go dim as the humming ceased. He racked his memory, reviewing every type of weapon with which he was familiar, every kind he'd ever read about in the Family library. A gun fitted with a silencer was relatively quiet, but a bullet inevitably left a wound, even when fired by handguns of the smallest caliber. A bow and arrow were lethal and silent, but an arrow invariably made entry and exit holes. Tiny darts, in the hands of an expert, could be fatal, but again, they produced discernible points of penetration. Poison seemed highly unlikely. How would Aloysius administer a toxin to an unwilling recipient?

The mystery was even deeper.

How were the victims in the locked rooms killed if the doors and windows were secured?

Did Aloysius own keys to all the buildings at the Complex? Or did the King possess a single key capable of unlocking almost any door?

Rikki remembered reading about a certain sort of key used by the criminal element prior to the Big Blast. A skeleton key, or passkey, it was called.

Did Aloysius own a skeleton key?

There were so many questions, and not enough answers.

So what was his next move?

Rikki jumped from the edge of the stage to the floor and headed for the red door, pondering his course of action. He gazed at the door, idly wondering why the King hadn't bothered to lock it. But why should Aloysius bother? The Hounds and the residents of Memphis were undoubtedly all terrified of the Dark Lord. Not one of them would be foolhardy enough to venture into the Dark Lord's chamber. Aloysius had devised the perfect deterrent, the ideal protector, and the irony of the situation was that the people of Memphis were subservient to an illusion. They were afraid of a shadow cast by a deranged mind. They were allowing themselves to be deluded because they lacked the courage to confront their fear, to face the truth.

He stopped in the doorway and looked back. What would happen, he wondered, if the people found out about the King's deception? Would they rise in rebellion and overthrow his despotic yoke? Would they put an end to his demented drive to conquer the world? Or would they still follow Aloysius, staking their survival on a planet torn by strife and chaos in a man whose mind was a reflection of the postwar devastation?

Rikki took a step into the throne room.

Just as the drumming cadence of many boots sounded from the corridor on the far side.

Aloysius the First must be returning!

And he had forgotten to close the throne room door!

CHAPTER NINETEEN

The man with the neatly trimmed beard scrutinized the Warriors. "Allow me to introduce myself," he said. "I'm Aloysius the First." He grinned maliciously. "The King."

Blade glanced at the corner they had just turned, then at the Hounds. He might be able to reach cover before they could fire, but he would endanger Chastity and Bonnie in the process.

"If you try anything," Aloysius declared, looking at the giant and the man in buckskins, "I will have the girl and Bonnie shot where they stand."

"I could plug this varmint before they get me," Hickok mentioned softly, so only Blade, Bonnie, and Chastity could hear.

"No," Blade responded. "We can't take the chance."

"What are you whispering about?" Aloysius demanded.

"We were wonderin' how someone with a face like a horse's butt got to be the head honcho around here," Hickok replied.

The King grinned. "Enjoy your petty witticisms while you can. The Dark Lord will put an end to your sarcasm."

"You're a brave man when you're backed up by three or four dozen guns," Hickok remarked. "How about you and me going at it, one on one?"

"Surely you jest?"

"Not in public," Hickok retorted.

"I have no need to prove my courage," Aloysius stated.

"In other words, you're a wimp," Hickok declared.

Aloysius glared at the gunman. "For that insult, you will die first."

"Good. I get bored just sittin' around," Hickok said.

"Drop your weapons!" Aloysius snapped.

"I'd rather not," Hickok answered.

"One word from me, and you'll be shot so full of holes that your own mother wouldn't recognize you," the King warned.

"At least I had one," Hickok cracked.

"Enough!" Aloysius barked. "Drop them now!"

Hickok looked at Blade. "It's your play, pard."

Blade unbuckled the gunbelt to the Smith and Wessons and allowed them to slip to the asphalt.

"Blast," Hickok muttered. He did the same with the Colts.

"Don't forget your knives," Aloysius said to Blade.

Frowning, the giant laid his big knives beside the gunbelt.

Hickok and Bonnie deposited their automatic rifles.

The King appeared to relax somewhat. He beamed expansively and approached them, with ten of the Hounds shadowing his every step. "There. That wasn't so hard, was it?"

"How did you find us?" Bonnie inquired.

"Elementary, my dear," Aloysius said. "When we lost contact with the platoon General Thayer dispatched, I knew you were on your way into the city. And when one of our squads failed to report in earlier, my hunch was confirmed. All of our patrols keep in touch with walkie-talkies." He paused, puffing out his chest. "I'd already decided to capture you myself, since the general has become unexpectedly lax in the performance of his duties. And when a patrol radioed in a report of a gunfight, I closed in on this area. I sent men up on the rooftops with binoculars. The rest was child's play."

"You're holding a friend of ours," Blade declared. "Where is he?"

"Do you mean the cute little man who likes big swords?"

"Where is he?" Blade reiterated.

"Rikki is a guest at my mansion," Aloysius said. "You'll be joining him shortly." He motioned with his left arm, and a couple of Hounds came forward and collected the weapons from the ground.

"Are you a bad man?" Chastity interjected to everyone's surprise.

Aloysius grinned at her. "Why, my dear child. Why would you ever say such a thing?"

"You took my Uncle Rikki."

"Rikki is your uncle?" Aloysius asked.

"In a manner of speaking," Hickok replied for her.

"What are your names?" the King inquired.

"Guess," Hickok said.

"I'm Chastity," revealed the six year old. "This is my new daddy, Hickok. And this" —she pointed at the head Warrior—"is my Uncle Blade."

"What a fount of information you are," Aloysius said sweetly. "Where are you from?"

"I'm from Atlanta," Chastity divulged. "My daddy and Uncle Blade are from far, far away. They live at the Home."

"Is that so?" Aloysius responded. He studied the Warriors. "Where might your Home be?"

"Mars," Blade answered.

"I'll learn the truth eventually," Aloysius vowed.

Hickok moved over to Bonnie and took Chastity. "Don't tell this cow chip anything else," he instructed her.

"I'm sorry. Did I do wrong?" Chastity asked.

"Just let me do the talkin'," Hickok advised.

Aloysius the First looked over his right shoulder. "Captain Tuchman, bring up the trucks."

A Hound officer saluted and wheeled, jogging off.

The King shifted his attention to Bonnie. "I can't begin to convey my disappointment in you. And after all we've meant to each other."

"Screw you!" Bonnie snapped.

"Again?" Aloysius said, and laughed.

"I'll never feel clean again," Bonnie commented bitterly.

"Aren't you being just a little melodramatic?" Aloysius queried. "After all, you were treated fairly."

"Fairly!"

"You accepted a formal invitation to my estate. You willingly indulged yourself at my table. And you were paid in gold for your company. It's not my fault you wouldn't accept my token of gratitude."

"I hate you," Bonnie stated.

"Hate me all you want. The fact remains that my conscience is clear."

"You don't have a conscience, you pig."

"Am I the pig? You ate like one, my dear." Aloysius chuckled. "I thought your stomach was a bottomless pit."

"If it's the last thing I ever do, I'll kill you," Bonnie asserted.

"Alas, dear heart, such a luxury will be denied you," Aloysius said. "By sunset you will be dead."

Blade listened to their conversation while assessing the possbility of escaping. He saw the two Hounds carry his Bowies and the other arms to the jeep on the left and place the weapons on the passenger side. The captain had reached the next intersection and was waving his right arm.

Seconds later, two convoy trucks lumbered into view from the left and turned toward the assembled Hounds.

"So you're the one who thinks he's going to conquer the world?" Blade inquired to take the heat off Bonnie.

"I don't think I will," Aloysius corrected him. "I know I will."

"Have you counted your marbles lately?" Hickok asked.

"Scoff if you like. Great men are always derided by those of lesser attributes," the King declared imperiously.

"You can't seriously expect to rule the world?" Blade said.

"As I told your friend Rikki, my goal is practical and achievable. I intend to gather to my banner all of the scavengers, raiders, and outcasts in the Outlands. My army will be unstoppable. The Hounds of Hades will destroy all opposition. Mark my words. I will rule the world.''

Hickok looked at Blade. ''Why do folks let themselves be bossed around by turkeys like this?''

''I rule because of my inherent superiority,'' Aloysius said.

Blade sighed. ''I've met men and women like you before. Tyrants who believe they have the right to impose their will on everyone else.''

''I do.''

''You'll be stopped. Tyrants come and go. Many have tried to set themselves up as supreme rulers over the centuries, and none have succeeded. Decades before the war there was a man named Hitler who tried to conquer the planet. He was defeated, and he had a vast army at his disposal. You'll suffer the same fate.''

Aloysius snickered. ''We shall see.'' He glanced at the convoy trucks as the vehicles stopped behind the jeeps. ''I must insist that you accompany me to my estate. I have a little surprise in store for you.''

''I like surprises,'' Chastity commented.

''This will be a surprise you'll never forget,'' Aloysius informed her. He gestured with his right hand. ''Would you be so kind as to board the trunk on the right? My men will escort you.''

Blade walked toward the truck, his skin tingling as the Hounds parted so he could pass. Dozens of rifles were still trained on him from adjoining roofs and windows, and he hoped none of the Hounds would get careless and prematurely squeeze a trigger. As he stepped past the jeeps he glanced at his Bowies, repressing an impulse to grab them and start swinging. Now was not the time. He moved around the truck to the rear, ringed by Hounds every foot of the way.

Captain Tuchman, a lean officer with a prominent nose and full cheeks, nodded at the open tailgate. ''Climb on board,'' he directed.''

Blade reluctantly complied, striding to the front and taking a seat on a narrow wooden bench running the length of the transport.

Hickok, Chastity, and Bonnie joined him.

"Well, this is another fine mess we've gotten ourselves into," the gunman groused as he sat down.

"Cheer up, Daddy," Chastity offered. "We'll be okay."

"I never should have led you back here," Bonnie remarked with remorse.

Hounds were clambering into the convoy truck and sitting on the bench. There was another bench on the opposite side, and both were quickly filled. Captain Tuchman was the last to climb on. "Don't try anything foolish," he called to the Warriors.

Hickok gazed glumly at a Hound involved with raising the tailgate. "They took my Colts. I don't like it when somebody takes my Colts."

Blade gripped the edge of the bench and stared at the floorboards. "We'll make our move when we find Rikki."

"Do you have a plan?" Bonnie asked in a low tone.

"Are you kiddin'?" Hickok rejoined. "My pard always has a plan." He looked at Blade. "You do have a plan?"

Blade nodded.

The gunman grinned and leaned closer. "You can count on me to back your play when the chips are down," he whispered. "What's your plan?"

"We go down fighting."

Hickok straightened, his forehead creasing. "That's it?"

"That's it."

"What kind of chicken doo-doo plan is that?" Hickok queried in disbelief.

"It's the best I can do on the spur of the moment."

Hickok snorted. "Brother! And Geronimo says *I* come up with cockamamie plans! Wait until he hears about this."

"Our only hope is to take out the King," Blade said quietly. "Maybe, just maybe, if we can kill him, the Hounds will fall apart. Without his leadership, there's no one to hold them together."

"You're forgetting the Dark Lord," Bonnie reminded him.

"Do you think the Hounds will follow the Dark Lord?"

"I know they will. They're scared to death of him," Bonnie said. "The Dark Lord might take over the Hounds if the King is wasted."

"Then Hickok will dispose of the King, and I'll handle the Dark Lord," Blade proposed.

"What about me?" Bonnie asked.

"You'll get Chastity out of the line of fire," Blade stated.

"But I want to help you."

"You're helping us by saving Chastity," Blade whispered. "We can't protect her and fight effectively at the same time."

"All right. I'll do it."

Blade glanced around. The nearest Hounds were seven feet off, and several were obviously attempting to overhear the conversation. "Wait for my signal," he directed his companions.

The rest of the ride was conducted in silence except for the rumbling of the truck motor and the creaking of the transport when the tires struck ruts and potholes. None of the Hounds spoke. Traveling to their rear, visible over the top of the tailgate, was the second convoy truck.

Blade thought of his wife and son, wondering if he would ever see them again, or any of the Family for that matter. He was growing weary of the constant trips to investigate reports of potential threats to the Home or the Federation. The run to Miami had devolved into a nightmare with the three Warriors being stranded over a thousand miles from their loved ones. He wanted to live to see them once more, to hold them in his arms. He wanted a vacation from his responsibilities, time off to enjoy life. Time, as the cliche went, to smell the roses.

The longer he dwelled on their capture, the madder he became. Why couldn't everyone live in peace and harmony? Why did the Spirit allow violence and hatred to exist? Oh, he was familiar with the teachings of the Elders. The Spirit, they proclaimed, was not responsible for the violence in the world. Humankind was endowed with free will, and the fate of the planet was in human hands. If humanity wouldn't accept the guidance of the Spirit and learn to value peace as the ideal standard of existence, then humanity must experience the consequences. Wars had plagued mankind throughout the course of history, and they would continue to do so for as long as power-mongers were permitted to spread hatred and violence. If those who really wanted peace were to prevail, they must be strong enough to eradicate every power-monger who appeared. Such was the price for free will. Such was the cost of universal brotherhood.

But what good did the knowledge do him?

All he wanted out of life was the opportunity to live happily with his family and friends and to live in peace with others. That was all any sane person wanted. Sanity, however, seemed to be in short supply on the planet Earth. Insanity was the order of the day. Sometimes, in his more philosophical moods, he even went so far as to imagine he was living on a cosmic insane asylum and the inmates were in control.

Aloysius the First was a case in point.

The man was clearly demented. Anyone with half a brain could see he was warped. Yet the people of this devastated city were following his every order. Why? How could they allow themselves to be blatantly manipulated? What prevented them from rising in rebellion? The Dark Lord? Was fear the only reason? Or was there a profound explanation rooted in fundamental reality?

At the moment, he couldn't care less.

He had a jeep stashed away, the means of transportation they needed to return to the Home. And the only thing standing in his way was a maniac with delusions of grandeur. The maniac, therefore, must be disposed of promptly.

The quicker, the better.

The convoy of trucks and jeeps wound through the city of Memphis, finally halting at the estate.

Blade heard muffled voices, then a grating sound, and the truck pulled forward. Peering over the heads of the Hounds, he saw a silver gate.

"We're here," Bonnie said, stating the obvious.

The truck drove up the drive to the front steps. Captain Tuchman stood. "All troopers out. Cover our prisoners."

With strict precision the Hounds jumped to the ground.

"Now you," Tuchman commanded the captives.

Blade rose and moved to the rear of the transport. He squinted in the bright sunlight, then stepped down.

Aloysius the First appeared on the steps. Behind him were two Hounds bearing the Bowies, Colts, and automatic rifles.

"Was your ride comfortable?" the King asked sarcastically.

Hickok slid to the asphalt with Chastity in his arms. "Go suck on a rotten egg," he answered.

"Crude. And very typical," Aloysius said. He looked at the officer. "Bring them, Captain."

Tuchman organized the Hounds into a column of twos. He hefted the M-16 he held and wagged the barrel in the direction of the front entrance. "Let's go," he directed the Warriors. "Take it slow."

Aloysius was ascending the steps.

Blade strolled toward the door, his arms at his sides, trying to convey the impression he was resigned to his fate. He wanted them unprepared when he made his move.

"Wow! This must be the biggest house ever," Chastity declared in amazement.

"I never wanted to set foot in this place again," Bonnie remarked apprehensively.

"Look at the bright side," Hickok suggested.

"What bright side?"

"One way or the other, this is the last time you'll need to come here."

"Thanks. I needed that."

"Any time."

Blade looked at the gunman. "Maybe you should give Chastity to Bonnie," he recommended.

"Good idea, pard," Hickok acknowledged, and kissed his newfound daughter on the right cheek. "You listen to

Bonnie, you hear? Do everything she tells you."

"I will," Chastity said.

Hickok handed her to Bonnie. "Take real good care of my young'un."

"No problem," Bonnie replied.

Hickok winked at Chastity, then caught up with Blade. "Say when," he whispered.

Blade nodded. He reached the top step and went inside, marveling at the plush interior.

"This way," Aloysius commanded, already a dozen steps up the wide stairway to the right. The pair of Hounds carrying the weapons were a step below him.

"I could never live in a place this size," Hickok commented as they started up.

"Why not?" Blade inquired.

"It's too blamed huge," Hickok said. "I'd get lost lookin' for the john."

Blade grinned, then looked over his left shoulder at the column of Hounds marching through the door. Captain Tuchman was covering them with his M-16. He faced front, climbing to the landing, scrutinizing the portrait of a man in black leather attire.

"Who do you think he was?" Hickok asked.

"I don't know."

"He can't be related to the King."

"Why do you say that?"

"He looks intelligent," Hickok quipped.

Blade turned the corner, trailing Aloysius and the two Hounds as they traversed another opulent corridor.

The King stopped abruptly, staring at an open door on the right-hand side. "That's odd," he remarked. "I know I closed it when I left."

The Warriors and Bonnie halted.

Captain Tuchman raised his right hand and the Hound column stopped.

Aloysius glanced at the officer. "Captain."

Tuchman hurried forward, past the Warriors. "Yes, sir?"

"Check my throne room," Aloysius ordered.

The Hound officer entered the chamber, and 30 seconds elapsed before he reappeared. "No one is here, sir."

Aloysius scratched his chin. "General Thayer must have been here and neglected to close the door. He'll be duly reprimanded for this gross oversight." So saying, he waved the officer out of his path and stalked inside.

"Let's go, you," Captain Tuchman instructed the Warriors.

Blade's eyes widened at the sight of the posters adorning the throne room walls. He gazed at the throne and the chandelier, and noticed a shut red door in the middle of the right-hand wall.

Aloysius stalked to his gilded throne and sat down. He beckoned for the prisoners to approach.

The column of Hounds tramped into the room and stood at attention, Captain Tuchman at their head.

"And now to business," Aloysius declared.

Blade gazed idly to his left at the duo holding the arms, then stared at the King. Hickok was to his right, Bonnie and Chastity a few feet to their rear. Behind them, the Hounds. "What do you propose to do with us?" he inquired.

"I could let the Dark Lord have you now," Aloysius said, and jerked his thumb in the direction of the red door. "But that would spoil all my fun."

"Where is Rikki?" Blade asked.

Aloysius gazed at the corridor. "I'm surprised he isn't here. I told General Thayer to bring him to the throne room before I departed to apprehend you. Perhaps the general returned your friend to his holding cell and went to find me." He smiled. "I can't wait to see the expression on that pompous Spartan when he learns I've captured you. He believes Spartans are such great military men! Well, they're not the only ones." The King chuckled. "I could have called him back, you know. He'd only been gone a couple of minutes, on his way to the cells to escort your friend here, when the word arrived of the gunfight. I decided to lead the

Hounds myself to demonstrate my superior ability, to show him my vision is valid."

"Vision?" Blade said.

"I'll explain later," Aloysius stated. "Right now I want to take a nice, long, hot bath and powder my face."

"Your puss could use some improvement," Hickok quipped.

Aloysius leaned forward. "How can you be so arrogant when you know that I have the power of life and death in my hands?"

"You don't have power over diddly," Hickok replied. "All you've got is the upper hand."

Blade looked at Bonnie and Chastity and observed them whispering. Bonnie lowered the child slowly to the floor.

"I intend to have you suffer before you die," Aloysius told the gunman. "I want to hear you beg for mercy."

"Don't hold your breath," Hickok advised.

The King snorted contemptuously. "You think you're so tough."

"I know I am," Hickok responded.

"Too bad you'll never have the opportunity to prove it," Aloysius said.

At that moment Chastity let out with a tremendous screech and raced toward the throne room door, swinging her arms and wailing. Bonnie took off in pursuit. "Chastity! Come back!"

Every Hound automatically focused on the screaming girl, watching her flee, some smirking at the sight. Even Aloysius glanced up in annoyance. For an instant no one was paying the slightest attention to the Warriors.

And Blade made his move.

The giant Warrior reached the pair bearing the weapons in a single stride. Before they could react, he wrenched the Bowies from the grip of the Hound bearing them and slid the knives from their sheaths with a deft flick of his hands. The gleaming blades flashed, and both Hounds were sliced across the throat in the space of a heartbeat. They released their burdens, clutching at their necks, blood spraying between their spread fingers, shock settling in.

Blade whirled and pounced on Captain Tuchman, imbedding his right Bowie in the officer's chest to the hilt. Tuchman's eyes widened in astonishment, and Blade yanked the knife free and shoved the collapsing officer aside.

Finally, belatedly, the Hounds began to come alive, several striving to bring their automatic rifles into play.

"No shooting! No shooting!" Aloysius the First unexpectedly shouted from his throne. "I don't want my posters hit! Use your bayonets and knives! Any soldier who uses his gun will answer to the Dark Lord!"

The Hounds hesitated uncertainly, torn between their duty and their desire to blow the giant away.

Blade seized the initiative, wading into the column with his Bowies arcing left and right, crimson droplets dripping from the blades as he hacked and cut, stabbed and slashed. Five Hounds were down in as many seconds. The next raised his AR-15, about to violate the King's order to preserve his life, but a booming retort sounded and the Hound's head was jerked rearward by the impact of a .357 Magnum slug tearing through his forehead. Blade managed a fleeting look back, elated to see Hickok entering the fray.

The gunfighter had retrieved his Colts.

Shouting and bellowing, the Hounds surged toward the Warriors, intending to overwhelm them by sheer force of numbers.

Hickok checked their rush, decimating their ranks with his Pythons, firing coolly, methodically, his elbows bent at the waist, his aim unerring, going for those nearest Blade. With each shot a Hound was flung to the floor. Ten of them perished as they dashed forward, falling at the feet of their comrades, throwing the Hounds into temporary disarray.

Blade wasn't about to allow them to reorganize. He glimpsed Aloysius the First darting through the red door out of the corner of his left eye, and then he attacked the remaining Hounds with the savagery of a primitive barbarian, his mighty physique rippling with power and ferocity, his conscious will supplanted by an instinctive drive to survive.

The Hounds tried to slay the rampaging titan, wielding their bayonets and knives as best they were able. A few decided to charge the gunman, thinking they could slay him before he could reload, but .357 slugs ripping apart their vital organs proved them wrong.

Blade was in his element, and he actually grinned grimly as he parried and thrust, blocked and struck. He felt stinging sensations in his arms, legs, and sides as he was nicked and cut, and he ignored the discomfort as he pressed his assault. A tall Hound attempted to spear his privates, and Blade impaled the man's neck on his left Bowie. Another Hound rashly sprang at his head, and Blade whipped his right Bowie into the soldier's groin, upending his foe with a powerful sweep of his steely arm.

Several of the Hounds opted to save their skins, turning and fleeing in stark panic. Two snapped off shots from their rifles. Both missed in the swirling melee of the battle, and both were promptly killed by the gunfighter in buckskins.

As he spun and shifted, always in motion, always the aggressor, Blade absently noted Bonnie and Chastity standing next to the wall near the entrance. They were transfixed by the violence unfolding in front of them.

Dead and dying Hounds littered the floor, moaning and groaning in torment, awash in puddles of their own blood.

Eight Hounds still fought on. One, a burly man with bushy eyebrows, turned and headed for the door, a bayonet in his left hand. He spotted the woman and child and angled toward them, his features contorting in fury. ''You did this!'' he roared.

Blade saw the Hound going after Bonnie and Chastity and stepped in their direction, but the seven Hounds circling him closed in, cutting him off. He renewed his onslaught, splitting a Hound's face with a slicing blow. ''Hickok!'' he yelled. ''Bonnie and Chastity!''

The gunman was already moving toward Blade, planning

to assist his friend. He quickly scanned the room, searching for Chastity and Bonnie, and spied them on the far side of Blade and the Hounds. The swirling flow of the combat prevented him from seeing them clearly, and he raced to the right, skirting the combatants, his blue eyes picking out his daughter and the woman just as a Hound reached them.

Bonnie, unarmed, defenseless, had pushed Chastity behind her, screening the child with her own body. She turned to confront the charging Hound, but he was on her before she could lift her arms to defend herself.

The burly Hound rammed his bayonet into Bonnie's abdomen, sneering in triumph as she gasped and doubled over. "Take that, bitch!" he cried, gloating. He looked down and saw the girl's terrified visage peering up at him from the shelter of the woman's legs. The child gazed past him and beamed in relief.

"Daddy!" Chastity shouted.

Tugging his bayonet loose, the Hound pivoted. Fear engulfed him at the sight of the gunman's countenance.

Hickok was pale, his mouth a thin slit under his mustache, as he stepped closer. The Colts were held steady, trained on the burly Hound.

"No!" the Hound said, extending his left hand, palm out. "No! Please!"

Hickok shot him, just once, the slug boring through the Hound's right kneecap and causing the soldier to buckle and fall onto his left knee.

"No!" the Hound bawled.

Hickok shot him again, planting a round in the Hound's right shoulder. The soldier twisted and almost went down, but he straightened with a determined effort.

"Please!" the Hound yelled plaintively. "Don't kill me!"

Both Pythons boomed.

The Hound was slammed onto his back, his mouth sagging, his eyes gone, replaced by the entry holes made as the slugs bored into his optic centers.

Bonnie was on her knees, bent down, her arms pressed

to her stomach, with Chastity crouched beside her.

Hickok glanced at Blade, noting the odds had been drastically reduced. Only three Hounds remained, and as he looked he saw one of those topple over, gutted like a freshly caught fish. He hurried to Bonnie's side and knelt. "Bonnie?"

She locked her eyes on his, conveying her misery and pain, her mouth trembling. "I'm scared to die."

"You won't die," Hickok said. "Let me see it."

"Don't bother," Bonnie declared, wheezing slightly.

Chastity moved to the gunman and draped her arms around his neck. "Help her, Daddy," she urged, tears streaking her cheeks.

Hickok leaned over for a better glimpse. All he could see was rivulets of blood and pale fluid seeping under Bonnie's folded arms and dripping onto the floor. "Move your arms."

"Forget about me," Bonnie said.

"I want to help."

"There's nothing you can do."

"You don't know that," Hickok stated, looking again at Blade.

One Hound left.

"I know," Bonnie replied with conviction.

"Do you want to stand?" Hickok asked.

"No," Bonnie said. "I'll stay right where I am." She grinned at Chastity. "You got yourself a real nice daddy. Don't let anything happen to him."

"I won't," Chastity pledged, sniffling.

"There must be something I can do," Hickok offered, feeling supremely helpless.

Bonnie shook her head feebly and sagged. "I never knew I could hurt so much."

"Are there any Healers in Memphis? I'll go fetch one," Hickok proposed.

"Too late," Bonnie mumbled.

A firm hand fell on the gunman's left shoulder and Blade squatted alongside him. "How is she?"

Hickok gazed at his friend, frowned, and shook his head.
Chastity began crying softly.

Bonnie gazed at the Warriors, grinning, blood dribbling
from the conrers of her mouth. "Did we kick butt or what?"

"We kicked butt," Blade said.

"The King?" she inquired.

"I'll get him," Blade vowed.

"You'll have to beat me to him," Hickok said.

Bonnie coughed and shivered. "Would one of you do me
a favor?"

"Anything," Blade said.

"Hold me. Please."

Blade knelt and cradled her shoulders tenderly in his arms.
"I'm sorry. I never intended for you to be hurt."

"My own fault," Bonnie responded. "I never did know
when to leave well enough alone." She coughed once more.
"I'm glad I met you two. I was beginning to think that all
men were only after one thing."

"Bonnie . . ." Chastity said.

"You be strong for your daddy," Bonnie stated. She
quivered and stared at the ceiling, her eyes glistening. "Oh,
God. I'm sorry I wasted it." And with that, she took a deep
breath and went limp.

"Bonnie!" Chastity screamed.

Blade lowered her body to the floor, then rose, simmering
with rage. He turned toward the red door.

Which abruptly opened.

CHAPTER TWENTY

Aloysius the First cackled as he closed the red door and secured a dead bolt located at shoulder level. He could hear the strident sounds of the battle, the cursing and clanging of blades and shrieks of agony. "Kill the bastards!" he muttered. "Kill them!"

How dare they defy his rule!

He backed away from the door in the darkness, absently running his fingers over the medals on his chest. "I'm the King. My will is law."

Shots thundered in the throne room.

"I ordered you not to fire!" Aloysius shouted at the closed door. "I don't want holes in my pretty posters."

"*Aloysius!*"

He spun, shocked to behold the fiery red eyes and the spheres of arcing light he knew so well.

"*I've come for you, Aloysius.*"

"This can't be!" he cried.

"*Your reign is over.*"

"This is impossible," Aloysius declared. "You can't talk without me."

"*Aren't I the Dark Lord?*"

The King took several strides forward, staring at the red orbs. "You're nothing without me! I created you to keep

my followers in line. I discovered the equipment in this room.
I'm your master.''

"The Dark Lord has no master."

Aloysius pressed his hands to his temples. "This isn't
happening. I'm hallucinating. That's it. I'm imagining the
whole thing.''

"This is real."

"No!" Aloysius responded, racked by a feeling of dis-
orientation. "I'm your creator. You don't exist without me.''

"You used me. You destroyed others in my name."

Aloysius clenched his fists and glared at the eyes. "Who
the hell do you think you are? I *made* you. I can use you
any way I want. So what if those imbeciles can't tell the
difference between a real mutant and a special-effects show?
So what if I convinced them I was being aided by an indes-
tructible mutant? I needed a method to force them to toe the
line, to obey me implicitly. You were perfect for the role.
An illusion can be as effective as reality if no one knows
the difference.''

"You killed."

"Of course I killed! I had to perpetuate the illusion. Don't
you see?''

"They will discern the truth eventually."

Aloysius tittered. "Those fools couldn't discern the truth
if they were sitting on it.''

"You were very clever."

"Damn straight I was!" Aloysius responded. He reached
into his right front pocket and withdrew the palm-sized,
metallic, tubular gun. "Do you see this? This is my ace in
the hole. No one knows I found this in the rubble of a
veterinary hospital. Do you know what it does? This fires
little needles. Thin, little needles. Coated with cyanide and
shot into the brain from close range, they kill within a minute.
No one knows that cyanide can be produced from common
items. But I do! I've read all about the process. There is a
book in a library in the suburbs . . . ." He stopped and tilted
his head.

*"So you used your needles to kill and spread fear among
your followers?"*

"You should know that."

"Did you use a key to enter locked rooms?"

"You should know that too."

*"And the one who was killed ten miles away? You tailed
him in another vehicle, wearing a disguise?"*

Aloysius touched his left hand to his forehead. "This can't
be happening. You should know all of this. You're me. I
mean, I'm you. I mean, we're both the same. So how can
I be talking to you when we're each other?"

"It is time, Aloysius."

"For what?"

"For you to pay for your deeds."

"I'm the master here!" the King yelled, and fired at the
blazing orbs.

Nothing happened.

"I'm coming for you."

"Stay where you are!" He fired again wildly.

"Reality has a way of catching up with you."

Aloysius sent another needle into the gloom. "I'm the
King! You will obey me."

The red eyes and the glowing spheres suddenly went black.

"What are you doing?" Aloysius demanded, looking from
side to side. "Where are you?"

The Dark Lord did not respond.

"Answer me!"

"I do this to protect my Family and all families everywhere," said a low voice from directly ahead.

"Who's there?" Aloysius snapped. "Who is it?"

"You can not be permitted to force your perversion on
others," stated the voice, only now the words emanated from
the left.

Aloysius swung in that direction. "I should know your
voice. I've heard it before."

"The spiritual must defend themselves from the bestial.

The sane must eliminate the psychopathically insane.'' This time the voice came from the right.

"Where are you?" Aloysius roared. "It's you, isn't it? The little man? Rikki?"

"Yes," was the response, spoken softly, seemingly arising from immediately behind the King.

Aloysius whirled, his finger on the trigger.

There was a sharp swish, a muffled grunt, and seconds later the thud of a body striking the floor.

CHAPTER TWENTY-ONE

They were walking hand in hand in the pristine eastern section of the Home, near the moat flowing at the inner base of the 20-foot-high brick walls enclosing the compound.

"Will Daddy be back soon, Mommy?" the boy asked. He was four months shy of his fourth birthday, and everyone in the Family agreed that he was the spitting image of his father: the same blond hair, the same blue eyes, and the same lean frame. He even wore a replica of his father's attire, buckskin pants and a buckskin shirt.

The woman looked away so he would not notice the sorrow lining her features. "I hope so, Ringo. I miss the big dummy."

"Daddy's not a dummy."

She glanced down at his earnest face and mustered a grin. "I know. I only call him a dummy because I love him."

"Does that mean I can call you a dummy?"

"Not unless you plan to cook your own food from now on."

"Does that mean no?"

"You're as bright as your old man."

"Are you sad, Mommy?" Ringo asked unexpectedly.

She did a double take. "Why do you say that?"

"I think you're sad because Daddy is gone."

"Aren't you?"

Ringo frowned and shuffled his moccasins. "Yeah. I reckon."

"Don't talk like that."

"Like what?"

"You know what I mean. Don't use the same kind of words your father does. He may like to talk like a turnip, but I'll be—darned—if you will."

"I think Daddy talks neat."

"You're the only one who does," she said, gazing to the north. They were slowly ambling toward the north wall, and the figure of one of her fellow Warriors, on guard duty, was visible on the rampart.

"Gabe and Cochise think Daddy talks neat too."

"They would."

"Why?" Ringo inquired.

She squinted up at the afternoon sun before replying, the heat prickling her skin, thankful she was wearing a light, green top and brown shorts with her deer-hide sandals. Strapped around her slim waist was a Smith and Wesson .357 Combat Magnum. "The three of you are chips off the old block—"

"What?" Ringo interrupted, not understanding.

"The three of you take after your dads," she stated. "You're just like Hickok. Gabe is Blade all over again. I never saw any boy eat as much and grow as fast as he's doing. And Cochise is exactly like Geronimo. Hickok, Blade, and Geronimo have been the best of friends since childhood, and I expect the three of you to follow in their footsteps." She paused. "The Spirit help us."

"What do you mean?"

"Your daddy has an uncanny knack for getting into hot water without really trying," she answered. "You'll probably be the same way."

"I hope so," Ringo declared.

"Just what I need," his mother muttered. She stared at the north rampart and recognized the Warrior. His muscular body was clothed in forest-green apparel. A six-inch strip of leather secured his shoulder-length blond hair in a ponytail, and his blond beard was trimmed in a jutting profile from his chin. He held a Ben Pearson compound bow in his right hand, and on his back was his quiver of versatile arrows. He saw her and waved.

"Yo, Sherry!"

"Hi, Teucer," she called back.

"Hi, Ringo," the bowman shouted. "How are you?"

"I miss my daddy."

Teucer glanced at Sherry, then back at the boy. "We all do, Ringo. Don't worry. He'll show up. Your dad always does."

"If he doesn't come soon, I'll go get him," Ringo declared solemnly.

"Speaking of which," Teucer said to Sherry, "what's the word from the Elders?"

"They still won't permit anyone to travel to Miami in the SEAL," Sherry said. "They want us to be patient."

"Any word on the missing jet?"

"No," Sherry replied. "We received a communique from the Federation Council. They have no idea what happened to the missing VTOL, but they suspect the Russians may have shot it down before it reached Miami to pick up Hickok and the others."

"Did they say why they suspect the Russians?"

"No. They promised a full report as soon as their investigation is complete."

"I hope you hear from them soon," Teucer commented.

"Not half as much as I do," Sherry replied.

Teucer nodded sympathetically, gave a little wave, and proceeded to the east.

Sherry led her son to the west, strolling past imposing pines, shafts of sunlight streaming between the trees.

"Mommy?" Ringo asked.

"Yes?"

"Why didn't Daddy and Uncle Blade take the SEAL?"

She gazed at him thoughtfully. The SEAL was yet another

of the legacies bequeathed to the Family by the Founder of
the survivalist retreat, Kurt Carpenter. Carpenter had spent
millions to have a unique mode of transportation developed
by the best scientists and engineers money could buy prior
to World War Three. The result had been the SEAL, a revol-
utionary, vanlike, solar-powered, all-terrain vehicle. The
Warriors utilized the SEAL frequently on their runs to
different destinations.

"Why not, Mommy?" Ringo repeated.

"Blade wanted to use one of the jets for several reasons,"
Sherry informed him. "First, the VTOLs are much faster
than the SEAL, and he wanted to get to Miami and return
as quickly as possible. Second, they'd cut down on the
number of mutants, wild animals, and whatnot they'd have
to face by taking a jet. Third, the VTOLs can land anywhere.
They have what's called a vertical-takeoff-and-landing
capability, so they can deposit the Warriors at any spot Blade
picks." She paused. "Blade thought he was doing the right
thing. We can't blame him for what happened."

"I don't."

"Good."

They strolled in silence for a couple of minutes, engrossed
in their private reflection.

Sherry raised her head as the sounds of shouting arose from
the western section of the 30-acre Home. While the eastern
portion was predominantly maintained in a natural state or
devoted to agriculture, and the central area was occupied by
a row of log cabins running from north to south, exclusively
reserved for married Family members and their children,
the western section was the focal area for Family socializa-
tion. Most Family activities transpired in the western sector.
The huge concrete blocks, each one exclusively reserved for
a specific function, were located there. In the middle of the
west wall was the only means of entering the compound, an
enormous drawbridge.

"What's that noise?" Ringo inquired.

"I don't know," Sherry said. "I hope it's not another

mutant.'' She hurried forward.

"Not so fast, Mommy," Ringo complained. "I can't keep up."

"Sorry."

Sherry scooped him into her arms and hastened onward, her pulse quickening, hope uplifting her emotions in a tidal wave of expectation. Despite her normal inclination to dread the worst, deep within the core of her being, sparked by her frequently accurate feminine intuition, was the conviction that Hickok was still alive, out there somewhere. The big dummy might attract trouble like honey attracted bears, but he also was endowed with lightning reflexes and could well be the quickest gunman alive. If anyone was capable of journeying great distances across the mutant-ridden landscape, he was.

Whoops and cries of delight were mingling in the air, muted but alluring.

"Someone is having a party," Ringo said.

"Maybe," Sherry responded, increasing her speed. Minutes later she reached a tilled field filled with growing corn, and she headed straight through, wending among the rows of stalks.

"Mommy?"

"What?" Sherry answered absently.

"When I grow up, I want to be a Warrior like daddy and you."

She looked into his innocent eyes and frowned. "We'll talk about this when you're older. A lot older."

"Can't I do it?"

"We'll see."

"Daddy and you are Warriors."

"I know."

"Why can't I be one?"

"I never said you couldn't," Sherry said.

"You don't want me to do it. I can tell."

"Being a Warrior is a very dangerous profession. Your

life is always on the line. I don't know if I'd want you to have a job where you might wind up being shot.''

''But you have the same job.''

''I'm your mother.''

''Aww, gee.''

''You're our only son, our only child,'' Sherry noted. ''I'm not about to agree to you having any position where your life is at risk.''

Ringo digested this information as they came to another tilled field, this one with a variety of vegetables.

Sherry bore to the left, not wanting to accidentally tread on any of the precious food.

''Mommy?''

''Yeah?''

''If the stork brings me a sister or brother, can I be a Warrior then?''

''A stork? Where did you hear babies are delivered by a stork?''

''From Daddy.''

''Figures,'' Sherry muttered. ''What did he tell you?''

''Do you remember when the horse had the baby horse?''

''Black Beauty, when she had her foal?'' Sherry asked, knowing he was referring to the delivery by one of the horses used by the Tillers.

''Yep.''

''What about it?''

''I asked Daddy where the baby horse came from,'' Ringo recounted. ''He said a stork brought it.''

''He did, did he?''

''Yep. And you know what else?''

''I can't begin to imagine.''

''Daddy said storks bring people babies too. Even deer babies and fox babies.''

''Busy bunch of storks,'' Sherry muttered. She estimated they were within a hundred yards of the line of cabins, drawing near to her own.

"And you know what else?"

"No, what?"

"Do you remember the animal books in the library?"

"The books you like so much, the ones with all the pictures?"

"Those books," Ringo confirmed.

"I asked Daddy where baby elephants came from," Ringo mentioned.

"And he said a stork."

"How did you know?"

"Just a lucky guess," Sherry commented dryly.

"But not little storks."

"Little storks?"

"Daddy says little storks bring little babies, like baby fish and baby birds. And madi—medu—"

"Medium?"

"Yep. Medium storks bring people babies. But elephant babies come from really big storks with beaks this big," Ringo detailed, and stretched his hands apart as far as they would go.

"I'm going to have a *long* talk with your father when he gets back," Sherry observed.

"Did you ever see a beak that big?"

"Just your daddy's nose."

Ringo laughed at the notion. "Daddy's nose isn't that big."

"It will be when I'm through with him," Sherry vowed. She was disappointed to note the uproar in the western sector had tapered off. A cluster of trees separated them from their cabin, and she bore to the left, following a well-worn trail.

The cabin came within view in seconds.

"Daddy!" Ringo exclaimed, kicking his legs in excitement.

Sherry froze in her tracks, her mouth slack, her green eyes watering.

"Let me down! Let me down!" Ringo yelled.

"Here you go," Sherry mumbled, lowering him to the ground.

The boy was off like a shot, running toward his father,

shouting with delight. "Daddy! Daddy! You're home!"

"I'm home," Hickok replied, standing six feet from the open cabin door. He beamed and knelt, his arms wide, and a moment later Ringo plowed into him and nearly knocked him over. "I'm home, buckaroo."

Father and son hugged one another, Hickok with his eyes closed, Ringo giggling and saying over and over again, "You're back! You're really back."

"And I'm not leavin' for a spell," Hickok stated. "I promise." He opened his eyes to find Sherry in front of him, her eyes and cheeks moist, and he kissed Ringo and stood. "Howdy, ma'am. Did you miss me?"

"No," Sherry said, then threw herself into his arms, her face pressed against his neck. "Don't you ever do this to us again!"

"I didn't exactly plan it," Hickok remarked huskily.

Sherry sighed and kissed him tenderly on the neck. "Dear Spirit, how we missed you!"

"You needed someone to help with the dishes, huh?"

Sherry chuckled. "You know you'll do anything to get out of doing work around the house."

"Who, me?"

"No. The storks."

"The what?"

"We'll talk about it later," Sherry said.

"Uhhh," Hickok began sheepishly. "There's something we need to talk about right now."

Sherry leaned back and pecked him on the tip of his nose. Ringo was squeezing the gunman's right leg. "Whatever is it, I'm sure it can wait," she stated.

"I'm afraid it can't," Hickok replied.

"What is it?"

"Promise you won't get all riled?"

Sherry's eyes narrowed quizzically. "Uh-oh. What have you done now? Whenever you say that, it means you've gone and done something off the wall." She grinned. "Men are so predictable. And here I am, outnumbered in my own family.''

Hickok cleared his throat, his mouth twisting in a cockeyed, reserved grin. ''Not any more.''

''What do you mean?''

''I brought you a little surprise,'' Hickok said.

''Oh?'' Sherry smiled. ''You've never done that before. What is it? Jewelry? Clothes?''

''Do you remember telling me that you'd like our next young'un to be a girl?''

''Yeah. So?''

Hickok nodded at the cabin.

Perplexed, Sherry looked, and the sight of the blonde girl wearing a blue jump suit, framed in the doorway, caused her to release her husband and step back in astonishment. ''Who—?'' she blurted out.

''This is Chastity,'' Hickok introduced the child. ''Chastity, this is Ringo,'' he said, and patted his son on the head. ''And this is Sherry, my missus.''

Chastity walked over to them, her anxious gaze on Sherry. ''Will you be my new mommy?''

''Your mommy?''

''My mommy and daddy were killed,'' Chastity explained with naive simplicity. ''My new daddy said you would be my new mommy.''

Sherry, still stunned and confused, squatted. ''Your new daddy?''

Chastity pointed at Hickok. ''He said you're the nicest lady in the world. He said I could be your girl.''

''How about it?'' Hickok asked. ''Look at the bright side. You won't have any morning sickness this time.''

''Where—how—when—?'' Sherry began, and then discerned the unease, the incipient fear, in Chastity's eyes. She reached out and impulsively embraced her. ''Don't worry. Everything is all right.'' She paused, watching tears form in the corners of Chastity's eyes. ''You've found a new home. Yes, I'll be your new mommy.''

''Thank you,'' Chastity stated politely, and started crying.

"What's wrong, princess?" Hickok inquired as he lifted Ringo in his arms. "I figured you'd be happy."

"I am," Chastity blubbered.

Sherry clasped the girl and stroked her hair. "There. There. It's okay." She glanced up at Hickok, and for an instant her eyes seemed to reflect all of the love in the world.

"Wow, Dad. Thanks," Ringo said.

"For what?"

"Now I can be a Warrior."

"Fine by me," Hickok responded, and gazed at each of them in supreme happiness. "How about this? Everything has worked out just fine." He paused. "Now I won't have to help with the dishes any more."

"Dream on," was Sherry's reply.

In the western section of the compound, not far from the lowered drawbridge and the dusty jeep parked a dozen yards from the moat, purposely avoided by the other Family members to allow them some measure of privacy, stood Blade, Jenny, and Gabe. They were embracing tenderly, not even speaking, simply savoring their reunion, with Jenny weeping softly, Gabe sniffling, and Blade feeling an overwhelming sense of sheer joy.

Thirty feet to the north, partially obscured by a towering pine, oblivious to everyone and everything as they kissed passionately was the Family's preeminent martial artist and a red-headed woman wearing a yellow blouse and brown pants.

"I never want you to leave again," she said when they came up for air.

"I'm a Warrior, Lexine. I must leave when Blade orders me to do so."

"I love you so much, Rikki."

"And I love you."

"Don't you think it's about time we did something about the way we feel?"

"I do," Rikki said.

"Then let's go find a clearing in the woods," Lexine suggested.

"I have a better idea," Rikki proposed.

"What is it?"

"Will you do me the honor of becoming my wife?"

A poor red squirrel, busily gnawing on a pine cone on a limb 25 feet overhead, nearly lost his footing and fell at the sound of a screech from one of the two humans below. He chittered at them for a minute, then scampered higher to enjoy his meal of pine seeds in peace.

**In the beginning, there was *Endworld*.
Now, there's...**

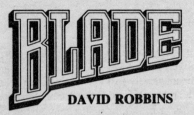

DAVID ROBBINS

The high-action companion series to *Endworld*.

The hero of Leisure's post-nuclear adventure stars in a new series that packs more power than an H-bomb. Named for the razor-sharp Bowies that never left his side, Blade was the last hope for a ravaged civilization.

BLADE #1: FIRST STRIKE
____2760-7 $2.95US/$3.95CAN

BLADE # 2: OUTLANDS STRIKE
____2774-7 $2.95US/$3.95CAN